A Matter of
PERCEPTIONS

A Matter of
PERCEPTIONS

J.L. Anderson

First Printing: February 2026

Paperback ISBN: 978-1-955541-83-1
Hardcover ISBN: 978-1-955541-84-8
eBook ISBN: 978-1-955541-85-5

LCCN: Pending
Author Headshot by Leslie Haney

Cover and Interior Design: FuzionPress

Published by FuzionPress
1250 East 115th Street, Burnsville, MN 55337

To my husband, Wade.
My rock.

With special thanks to
Lindsay Vaughn and Alex Anderson.

CHAPTER 1

Fiona sat on the edge of the bed and leaned into the fan, lifting her top so the blowing air could cool her glistening skin. Even at this early hour the temperature was nearing ninety degrees. The *least* he could have done was get her an apartment with air conditioning, she groused. She bent down, picked up the fan, pulled the fan plug from the wall, and trudged to the bathroom. She placed it on the little dresser, plugged it in, and turned it to high. She drew her unnaturally bright auburn hair up into two short messy pigtails to get them off her neck revealing the strands of purple underneath. Even this small effort caused beads of perspiration to appear on her forehead. She grabbed a towel and wiped her face. *Damn this heat.*

She opened the folding closet doors revealing all her clothing creations – each piece unique. She reached in and chose one she knew he hated. She slipped it on and smiled at herself in the mirror. Soon, very soon, she thought to herself.

Throwing the towel over her shoulder, she picked up her laundry bag and satchel, stepped out of the apartment door and locked it. She opened the vestibule door and looked both ways for any seedy characters who might be hanging about or students who partied too hard, sleeping in the yard. Steam rose from the asphalt and she could feel the heat of the pavement through the bottoms of her newly decorated high top tennis shoes as she walked down the sidewalk. Street parking near the University was hard to come by – especially when you arrive home late at night. Last night she had to settle for a spot three blocks down. It was just another thorn in her side. The jerk wouldn't even *consider* an apartment with underground parking.

She crossed the road to her car and dropped the laundry bag on the dead, brown grass next to it. She opened the driver's side door releasing the sweltering air from inside. It was a sauna in there. She opened the door to the back seat to increase the air flow, then plopped down on her laundry bag and sighed. No way was she getting into that kiln of a car. How she hate, hate, hated the heat. *Damn him.*

After only a few minutes in the sultry sun, Fiona decided it was just about as hot on the outside as it was on the inside. She stuck her head back in the car. A drop of her sweat fell onto the seat and practically sizzled. Not a great choice here, she thought to herself, but she'd have to tolerate it. She tossed the laundry bag onto the passenger seat, placed the towel on the front seat, and carefully sat down on it making sure not to let her skin touch the still blistering-hot Naugahyde. She started the car, opened all the windows, and turned the fan on full. She put the car in drive and let the air blow across her face. *That was better.*

She took the entrance onto Highway 94 and merged into the traffic. It was light on a Tuesday morning, so it didn't take long to reach her exit. She turned right down the parkway, then left down his street where all the rich people lived. She eased down the long driveway, opened the garage, and parked in her usual spot. It would be nice to get out of the heat and into his air conditioning for a while. She stepped through the door to the back hallway and allowed herself one short moment to revel in the cool, filtered air.

There was plenty to accomplish today, but first things first. She chucked the laundry bag by the washer and made a beeline for the main bedroom. She knelt down next to the bed and peered under the mattress. Plenty still under here, she thought with delight. She took several bundles, made a quick trip out to her car, and hid them in the trunk. That would keep her for a while.

It was four years ago that Fiona happened upon his stash of cash. He had berated her for what he called a "half-assed" job cleaning, then ordered her to do it again. "You've got to pull your own weight around here. You're just plain useless. I'm not going to just hand you money on a silver platter," he had said to her, along with the other more colorful expletive tongue-lashings Fiona had heard all of her life. So in retaliation, she decided to slip his Ferrari key fob under his mattress where she thought he'd never find it.

That's when Fiona discovered his cache. She quickly decided not to hide his fob, but instead helped herself to a little bit of the money. He never noticed, so a couple weeks later she took some more, and even more the next. If he had ever found out, she would have been dead meat, but that was a chance she had been willing to take.

It had always been that way with their relationship. At least as far back as she could remember. He didn't care for her, and he let her know it. She was a burden, his load to bear, a pain in his ass, a black hole for his money. He could go on and on like this.

Perhaps his history gave an excuse for his behavior, but even so, that didn't mean his words didn't hurt her to her core. Besides, she had essentially the same history - except the abandonment part. She wasn't sure why, but his mom just up and left when he was a small boy. No note and never any explanation. Just gone one day. A few years later, his dad remarried, and a few years after that, Fiona was born. When she was eight years old, her mother (his step-mother) died suddenly, and then their dad lost the farm to the bank. Dad ended up hanging himself in the hen house. So, her then eighteen-year-old brother, Artie, went off and joined the army, and Fiona went to live with her mother's sister, their only still-living relative. Fiona and Artie were reunited when he came home a military hero. After that, he begrudgingly took her on, and she was told to be grateful for it.

Moving through the house she wiped, dusted, washed, scrubbed, scraped, and polished until all was spotless inside. She could hear his voice inside her head, "Get going slacker! Beat feet! I want to see my face shining in it! I want to be able to bounce a coin off of it." Artie always wanted it cleaned to military standards. Today it would be so.

When the cleaning was complete, she took one last look around the house making sure nothing had been missed, then stopped at the sliding glass door to the back. She could feel the scorching heat on the windowpane. The backyard pool's water sparkled in the sun. She watched as a lawn chair floated across and bumped against the side. She sighed. She knew she had to go out there.

Dreading it, she took a deep breath of the air-conditioned air, pulled open the slider and stepped onto the concrete pad. She could hear the neighbors' children happily splashing about in their own pool. They didn't have a care in the world. How she envied them. She walked to the side of the water, reached out for the lawn chair, pulled it aside, then lingered a moment, peering through the ripples at the large, pale mass at the bottom of the pool.

CHAPTER 2

What in the world was all of this, Isaac thought to himself as he turned onto Fremont Avenue. He slammed on the brakes to avoid hitting a man who ran right out in front of him and crossed the road without any regard for his own safety. News station vans lined both sides of the avenue and the area was inundated with people sprinting down the street, the sidewalks, and across the lawns carrying their microphones and cameras, with sweat flying off their foreheads as they went. So many, in fact, Isaac was unable to count them. It was like a news media Kentucky Derby.

There was always some curiosity when a body was found, but this? This was not normal. Just who's passing would muster this much attention, he wondered.

Isaac turned on the lights hidden inside the front and back windows of his unmarked police car. The bright blue and red strobes began flashing, catching the attention of the multitude of reporters blocking his path, silently ordering them to move their news vehicles and equipment out of the way.

While the drivers of those news vehicles jostled with each other to capture the most advantageous spots, Isaac took the opportunity to scan his surroundings. The homes in this area of Minneapolis were massive and well-tended. Only the wealthiest, whether by the inheritance of family money or their own hard work and ingenuity, could afford to live here. Could this have been a burglary gone terribly wrong? A family dispute? Whatever the cause, the victim had to be a mogul of society, because in addition to the throng of reporters on the ground, news helicopters hovered overhead. And despite the oppressive heat, the streets were teeming with neighbors who came out of their air-conditioned mansions to see what all the commotion was about. He watched as they crowded under the shade of the trees lining the road, holding their miniature fans up to their tanned skin to try to keep cool.

He ran a hand over his face. How he hated when someone of notoriety passed away 'unexpectedly.' The press would be hounding Captain Petruco, and Captain

Petruco would be hounding him. He took a deep breath, bracing himself for what lay ahead. Never in his entire career as a detective — and he had been at this quite a long time — had he seen this much interest in a drowning. It wasn't helpful.

Neither was a certain well-known female reporter who, despite Isaac's quiet mandate to clear the road, continued her play by play right in the middle of the street blocking his path and making all the other reporters angry. He could hear them grouse even through the tightly closed windows of his vehicle with the air conditioning running on high.

"Hey, why is *she* still out there?" one reporter complained.

"Get out of the road, Mimi!" another called. "Can't you see an officer is trying to get through?"

Isaac watched the pandemonium for a few minutes, patiently waiting for her to wrap up, but it became clear she had no intention of doing so as her high heels sank deeper into the hot pavement. He tapped gently on his horn. She didn't seem to notice. He pulled in closer. The red and blue lights flashed across her body like she was at a disco. She didn't budge. He tapped his horn again. Still no movement or even an acknowledgement that he was there. He inched up even closer, so close, in fact, he had to believe his car was now part of her broadcast. To his astonishment, she still wouldn't leave.

He hadn't intended on using it because it was just so annoying, but then, so was this reporter. He reached over and flipped the switch. The loud pitch of his siren blared causing said reporter to literally jump out of her shoes — arms flailing and hair flying. It was quite a sight. Isaac pursed his lips together to keep from bursting with laughter. The others in attendance were not so kind, and an eruption of cheers and applause filled the air as the startled reporter gathered herself, plucked her stilettos from the pavement, and stormed off.

His way now clear, Isaac turned off the siren and maneuvered his vehicle through the narrow corridor, grinning from ear to ear. He pulled up to the barrier at the top of the driveway and rolled down his window. The oven-hot air poured in. "What's all this, Bill?" he yelled to the officer at guard.

"We've got a drowning," Bill yelled back from under the shade of the large maple tree hanging over the entrance.

Isaac laughed. "I know that, Bill. That's why I'm here." He gestured widely. "That's why we're all here."

Bill ambled over to the side of Isaac's car. The armpits of his shirt were wet and his forehead was glistening. "Crazy right? It's some famous guy I've never heard of."

"Is that so." Isaac pointed his thumb back over his shoulder. "Bill, would you please make those news crews keep their vehicles and reporters to the sides of the road so traffic can get through?"

Bill pulled at the moist collar of his shirt. "Isaac, I'd love to." He gave the van to his right a hostile stare. "Those vultures." He shook his head. "But we're short staffed right now – and I was specifically told that guarding the driveway was most important, so here I am." He slapped the hood of Isaac's car leaving a wet spot from the perspiration on his hand. "We've got more troops on the way, though."

"Okay, thanks. Open the barrier for me, will you?"

"My pleasure," Bill said.

Isaac passed through and gave Bill a wave. "Stay cool!"

It was a long driveway that meandered through forest-like property. The dark, green summer foliage filled the grounds. If this turned out to be a homicide investigation, it would take some effort to search it all. Hopefully that wouldn't be the case, but they'd need to wait for the Medical Examiner's report to be sure. In the meantime, they would treat it as if they suspected foul play.

The ambulance was parked next to the entry, and the firetruck was in a turnabout area in front of the garage, so Isaac decided to leave his car further up the drive to allow room for the other vehicles to exit.

He opened the door into a thicket of brush and pulled himself out of the car, being careful to disturb as little of it as possible, then made his way slowly down the driveway taking in the scene. Big, modern home. Landscaping that needed tending.

The front door swung open. "Isaac. We've been waiting for your arrival."

"Hi Vick," Isaac said. "I didn't expect to see you here."

"Petruco sent me." He slapped Isaac on the arm. "Your right-hand man is back!" He smoothed his hair back over his head looking like James Dean. He smiled that sly smile. "I'm all yours."

Vick was Isaac's last partner who decided Minnesota winters were just too much to bear and had moved off to California last February. It didn't last long.

"Okay. Fill me in."

Vick flipped open his note pad like it was a communicator on the starship Enterprise. "In a nutshell, the sister came to clean the house and saw a lawn chair floating in the pool. When she went to pull it out, she saw the victim at the bottom of the pool."

"Have you interviewed her?"

"Yeah, for a bit." He leaned toward Isaac's ear and put his hand to the side of his mouth. "She's been flirting with me all morning."

"Flirting with you?" Isaac rolled his eyes. Vick always thought women were flirting with him. Just one of the countless things Isaac had not missed while Vick was away in California. "Vick," he said, "You haven't changed a bit."

"Yeah, well. You know I just have that effect on women." Vick shrugged. "What're you going to do?" He grinned widely. "Just another day being me, I guess."

Isaac shook his head. "So where is she now?"

"The dusting crew came in, and she suddenly got queasy and asked to take a break and lie down."

"That's certainly understandable. We'll let her have some time. Where's the body?"

"Back by the pool. The divers just pulled him out." Vick led Isaac through the huge, open living space toward the back of the house. "But watch out," he added. "Cynthia's here."

"Good," Isaac responded. Isaac was probably the only one in the world who was ever happy to see Cynthia. She was a petite, sinuous woman with long, silky black hair, and on first glance, one might describe her as a sweet, little kitten, but upon meeting her, they'd discover she had the bite of an angry lion. Isaac had been hoping she'd be taking charge of this one. Drownings were the most complex cases and Cynthia was the best medical examiner on the staff.

They walked through the sliding glass door back into the hot summer heat. Isaac pulled at his collar. "Man, with this heat, I'm surprised the water in the pool isn't boiling."

"Ha!" Vick exclaimed. "This is nothing compared with California. It's probably over a hundred twenty degrees there now. I'll take this any day."

Cynthia was kneeling next to the body.

"Cynthia!" Isaac called.

Cynthia stood to her full height of five feet. "Isaac, I'm so glad you're here." She threw up her arms. "These imbecile divers dragged his body over the edge and now we'll have postmortem abrasions."

Typical Cynthia, Isaac thought to himself. If she wasn't complaining about something, he'd suspect something was terribly wrong. He looked over at the divers who were steaming in their suits. "I'm sure the divers were doing the best they could," he said.

She gave the evil eye to Vick. "And what is this idiot doing here? Where's Detective Bryant?"

"Detective Bryant is on vacation." And most certainly, Isaac thought to himself, Detective Bryant would be another one of those people who would be very happy not to have to work with Cynthia.

"Well, I hope he'll be back soon. I wouldn't want to leave this investigation up to sub-standard help," she said referring to Vick. "We're talking about the death of Artimus."

Vick shook his head at her and flipped open his note pad. "No Cynthia, the name is Artie Farkus," he corrected.

"You see what I mean?" She pointed her finger at Vick, arm fully extended. "He's already got it wrong. This is not just 'Artie Farkus.'"

"Well, that's the name the sister gave me," Vick responded indignantly. "I'd think she'd know her own brother's name, Cynthia."

"You moron. This is Artimus. *The* Artimus." She emphasized the word "the" and said it in the King's English. "Minnesota's Van Gogh. He's an international treasure.

Known by the entire *educated*, and culturally civilized world."

Vick rolled his eyes.

Isaac, not wanting to let on that he also had no idea who Artimus was, just said "Ohhh," in a way that sounded like he did.

Cynthia turned her attention toward the divers. "You're dripping all over the crime scene you idiots."

Isaac raised his brow. "Is it a crime scene, Cynthia?"

"Isaac, you know better than to ask such a stupid question. Drownings are a complicated business. I won't know until I rule out what didn't happen, will I?" She knelt down and tested the body for the state of lividity, then pressed on the deceased's chest. Bloody froth oozed out of his mouth and nostrils.

"Oh my God, what is that?" Vick asked.

"The extravasated blood resulting from alveolar capillary rupture," Cynthia explained as she took a sample. She lifted Artimus' hand and turned it over to see the shriveling. "Washerwoman's hands."

"I thought you said he was a painter," Vick said.

"Ugh!" She sat back on her heals and glared at Vick. "You nitwit! Washerwoman's hands is the wrinkling of palms, soles and fingers as a result of dermal absorption of water." She turned toward Isaac. "Isaac, would you please remove this idiot from my sight."

Vick straightened his collar and sneered at Cynthia. "I'll think I'll go check on sis," he declared and made his getaway to the air-conditioned home.

"And don't come back," she called after him. She turned her focus to the photographer. "Did you get all the photos?"

The photographer nodded.

"Don't just bob your head at me," she admonished. "Give me a clear answer. A spoken answer."

"Yes, Dr. Chu, I took all the necessary photographs."

"There. That's better." Cynthia performed a few more basic examinations, then pulled off her latex gloves. "Did we get the temperature of the water?" she called out to the team.

Having witnessed the photographer's berating, every-one, in unison, said "Yes, Dr. Chu."

"Okay, I'm going to estimate the time of death some-where between seven and nine o'clock last evening," she said. "Write that down," she told the team.

"Yes, Dr. Chu," they all responded as they scribbled in their note pads.

"Okay, let's get him on the gurney."

The team moved in.

"Carefully!" she commanded. "Remember, even fin-ger pressure can cause capillary damage and postmortem extravasation artifact! We can't allow those to affect the results of my examination!"

Once Artimus was bagged and placed on the gurney, Isaac entered the home to make way for the cart. "Please stand aside," Isaac asked the forensics team. "They're bringing the body out."

As the team began moving out of the way, Isaac noticed Vick and a young girl, who he assumed was the sister, emerge from the hallway ahead and decided to rephrase his request, "Please stand aside, people. They're bringing Mr. Artimus through."

"Isaac!" Cynthia scolded. "It's Artimus, not *Mr.* Artimus."

"Well yes, of course, Cynthia." Isaac said, then gestured toward the girl. "I was just trying to be respectful in front of the family."

"Just the single name Artimus, demands respect in and by itself," she said firmly.

"Of course it does," Isaac responded.

Cynthia pushed by him and stopped in front of the sister. She looked her up and down.

Isaac could see the disapproval in Cynthia's eyes.

"Are you the one lucky enough to be Artimus' sister?" She nodded.

"What's your name?" Cynthia asked.

"Fiona."

Isaac stepped up next to Cynthia. "Cynthia, Fiona's under a lot of stress at this time," he cautioned, hoping Cynthia would curb her penchant to offer what she considered helpful, but was most often unwelcome, advice.

"Fiona, I loved your brother's work. My condolences," Cynthia said, then she turned and fell in behind the gurney.

Isaac let out a sigh of relief, but it was premature. Cynthia stopped abruptly and turned back.

"Cynthia?" Isaac called after her.

She held up a finger. "Just a minute, Isaac. We're talking about Artimus' legacy here."

Isaac held his breath.

"The press will be hounding you," Cynthia told Fiona. "You should do your best to represent your brother properly. He deserves that respect." She looked her up and down again. "So, to that end, I'm going to give you some advice." She touched the end of Fiona's sleeve like it was a piece of garbage. "Go to Nordstrom's and get some help. You look like a stray cat who lost a knife fight with the glitter fairy." She shook her head. "Really. Get some help."

CHAPTER 3

Meredith glided through the front door of the brightly lit gallery sporting a ponytail that made her look like Malibu Barbie. "Good morning, Darcy! Thank goodness for air conditioning. It's blazing hot out there." She gestured gracefully toward the entry. "Let's move those easels back from the front windows. The sun is going to be beating in today and we can't have any fading issues!"

Darcy scrambled to her feet and straightened her too-tight seer-sucker skirt. "You're – you're early," she stammered. She glanced at the clock above the desk. "Really early." She shoved the papers into her drawer and ran a hand over her head. "I honestly didn't expect you to be here this morning."

Meredith picked up the mail in her in-box. "I'm hoping to take the afternoon off, so I needed to get in here pronto to take care of a few things." She smiled showing her perfectly white teeth. "My dearest love wants to take me to lunch today."

Darcy felt her blood pressure begin to rise. "You're seeing him again today?"

Meredith looked up from the mail. "Whatever do you mean? I see him every day."

Darcy dropped back into her chair. "Oh, you mean *Dirk*." She let out a long sigh. "I thought you were talking about, well, you know." She twirled her hand in the air as an overture to have Meredith finish the sentence, but she didn't. Darcy glared at her. "You know very well who I'm talking about, Meredith. The one you were with last night."

Meredith laughed. "You silly," she said. "He's not my dearest love. Only my sweet husband deserves that title."

"Then why in the world do you see the other one?" Darcy hissed.

Meredith sighed. Darcy was not one to hide her disapproval. In fact, she was quite vocal about it. But Darcy just didn't understand. This wasn't for sharing. This was Meredith's personal business, and had it not been for that letter, it still would be. "My dear, dear, Darcy," she said. "How many times are you going to ask me that?"

Darcy sat back in her chair and folded her hands in her lap. "Until I get a clear answer."

"A clear answer?" Meredith looked toward the ceiling, taking a long moment to consider her response. In its essence it was quite simple really, but also quite difficult to explain to Darcy. She took in a deep breath and let it out slowly. "Okay. Here it is." She held her palms to the sky. "I'm trying to fulfill a dream."

Darcy raised her eyebrows. "Your dream is to have an affair?"

Meredith put her hands on her hips. "I keep telling you, Darcy. It's not what you think it is."

Darcy grunted. "You know that's still not a clear answer, Meredith."

"I'm so sorry, Darcy," she said sincerely. "But I can't help that. Let's move on, please. I had a late night."

"I noticed," Darcy said, not yet ready to abandon the subject. "I got up at around ten and my car still wasn't there." How she ended up agreeing to switch cars with Meredith for Meredith's dalliances, she really wasn't sure. All she knew was that it kept her up and fuming all night long.

"I know. My apologies." Meredith bashfully shrugged. "This one took a little longer than usual."

"Longer than usual?"

"Yes."

Darcy raised her brows. "So, was there a problem?"

"Oh, no. It went well."

"It went well? That's it?"

"Well, yes," Meredith confirmed. "It went very well. Mission accomplished." She turned her attention toward the front windows. "But enough about that now. We've got work to do. Big event coming up! Would you mind getting that artwork moved back from the windows?" She let out a snort. "In this scorcher, I wouldn't be surprised if they started melting!"

Darcy crossed her arms over her chest. It wasn't going to be that easy to move on from this topic. She had some news of her own to share, and it wasn't going to be happy news for Meredith. "Okay, but…"

"If any of the artists saw their creations baking in the sun, they'd throw a fit," Meredith prattled on. "Artists can be so melodramatic."

"Sure, but…"

"And speaking of melodramatic," Meredith continued, "have you heard anything about Art yet this morning? I mean, *from* Art? I'm going to need to touch base with him before the art exhibition."

"No," Darcy replied. "He's probably sleeping off a hangover. But…."

"But of course." She wacked her forehead with the heal of her hand. "Why would I even ask?" She spun on a heel and headed toward her office.

Darcy held up her hands to stop her. "Before you go in there, I've got to warn you." Darcy grimaced. "You got another one."

Meredith's face turned ashen. "What?"

"I set it on your desk."

CHAPTER FOUR

Fiona watched open-mouthed as Cynthia followed the gurney to the ambulance. "What a bitch," she said to no one in particular.

"You can say that again," Vick agreed.

Isaac cringed. Vick had no filter.

"Right? What a bitch!" Fiona repeated with more gusto. "Who the hell is she? What's she doing here?"

"Her name is Cynthia Chu," Vick explained. "She's the medical examiner. But she thinks she —"

Isaac grabbed Vick by the arm, stopping him mid-sentence. "Fiona," Isaac said. "I'm Detective Isaac Scott with the Minneapolis Police Department. I'm so sorry for your loss."

Tears started to well up in her eyes.

Isaac couldn't tell if they were tears over the loss of her brother or because Cynthia disliked her dress, but he always tried to believe the best of people unless and until they proved him wrong.

"How could she say that? This is one of my best pieces."

Isaac nodded. "Yes, I'm sure it is." He gestured toward the seating area. "Let's go sit down, shall we?"

Fiona made her way across the room, plopped down on one of the leather recliners, dropped her over–sized satchel on the floor next to her, and clasped her hands tightly in her lap.

Isaac held tight to Vick's arm. "Vick, I need you to go check on the security around the property." Isaac knew from past experience that his questioning of Fiona would go much better without Vick's interference.

Vick raised his eyebrows. "Outside?"

"Yes," Isaac confirmed. "Around the perimeter."

Vick smoothed his hair back over his head. "In this heat?"

Isaac smiled. "It's nothing compared to California. Should be easy for you."

Vick shook his head. "I go away for six months, and this is how you welcome me back? Can't you get one of the uniforms to handle this?"

"Well no, Vick. You're the one I depend on to make sure it's done right."

"Oh fine," Vick grumbled. "If you put it that way." He pointed a finger at Isaac. "But you owe me one."

Isaac watched Vick plod toward the door, then took a seat on the couch near Fiona. He pulled a tissue out of his pocket and handed it to her.

"Thanks." Fiona wiped the tears from her eyes. "I didn't think that would affect me like that."

That was more like it. His heart went out to her. "You've had a harrowing day," Isaac responded. "It's certainly understandable given the circumstances."

"I mean, what do I care what she thinks?" She blew her nose. "This is one of my favorites."

Isaac sighed and sat back in his seat. "It's very nice," he lied.

"Right?"

Isaac nodded, even though he agreed with Cynthia's assessment. Aside from a couple nasty, strategically placed slashes in the material, it sparkled like something a six-year-old girl would love. It was a rather confusing contradiction of Disney princess meets Hellraiser Pinhead.

"I mean, she's obviously not my target market."

"Yes, no need to worry about that," Isaac said, certain that was true.

Fiona sat back in her seat. "Right," she affirmed to herself. "This is real art," she proclaimed. "Not like what Artie does."

Isaac leaned forward. "Not like what Artie does?"

Fiona looked up at Isaac. "No, I just mean it's *different* than what Artie does," she back tracked. She'd have to watch that. It would be in her best interest to make sure Art's paintings held their value, because it would all be hers now. She cocked her head at him. "Who did you say you are?"

"Isaac Scott. I'm the detective who will be working on this case.'

She scanned the room. "Where's that other guy?"

"Detective Marchese is taking care of security."

"Oh, okay." She bit her lip. "Detective Marchese. Will he be back?"

Isaac sighed. It did indeed look like young Fiona was taken with handsome Vick. And Vick was sure to let everyone know. "It is certain," Isaac assured her. "In the meantime, I'd like to ask you a few questions."

"Okay, but I already told Detective Marchese everything I could remember."

"I know, and I know this is an emotional time for you, but I'd like to ask just a few more."

She crossed her legs causing one of the slashes to reveal most of her upper thigh which sparkled with glitter. "Okay."

"Can you tell me about how you found your brother?"

"Like I told Detective Marchese, I saw a lawn chair floating in the pool, so I went to get it and saw Artie at the bottom. He wasn't moving.

"Then you called nine one one?

"Yes."

"Were you supposed to meet with Artie this morning?"

"Not really. I mean, I didn't know if he'd be here or not. I came to clean his house like I do every so often."

"You clean his house for him?"

"Yes." She smiled. "I like to do what I can to help out since Artie has been funding my new business," she replied, neglecting to mention that Art wasn't aware he was doing so, because she had neglected to tell Art that she hadn't attended classes for the last couple years and that the money he was giving her for her schooling was being used for other things. But, in her defense, she was certain that the money was better spent investing in her business plan.

"Your new business?"

"Yes, I'm opening up a boutique."

"Ah, of course," Isaac responded. "So, you and your brother were close?"

"Oh yes, very close," Fiona lied. "We're the only family we have."

"No other siblings?

She shook her head. "Nope."

"And your parents?"

"Art's mom departed when he was young. Afterward, Art's dad married my mom. They're both dead now too."

"My condolences," he said even though she seemed unaffected by these losses. "There's no one else? No other relatives? Aunts? Uncles? Cousins?"

Another head shake. "Nope. We're all that's left of the Farkus family."

Isaac raised his brows. Did he detect a bit of glee in that comment? "What kind of cleaning do you do for him?"

"Everything. I dust, vacuum, wash floors, dishes, do the laundry – you name it." Fiona smiled. "I want to take as good care of him as he has of me," she said sweetly, hoping Isaac would believe her.

"And you cleaned the house this morning before you found your brother?"

"Yes, everything is spotless – just the way he likes it."

Not what Isaac wanted to hear. This would make their investigation much more difficult without fingerprints, shoe prints, fabric fibers, or all the other little things that forensics usually find at a crime scene – if this did indeed turn out to be a crime scene. "When you were cleaning, did you notice anything unusual? Anything out of the ordinary? Anything that would lead you to believe there was someone here with Artie last night?"

"No. Nothing. There weren't even any dishes in the sink – and usually there's a ton." Art always left all his messes for her to clean up.

"No dishes?"

"Nope. But I figured he was out of town or something."

"But you said you were close. Would he usually let you know if he was out of town?"

She shifted in her seat. "Artie kind of did what he wanted. Sometimes he'd just up and go."

"Fiona, I'm sorry to have to ask you this, but is there anyone you can think of that would want to harm your brother?"

"Ha!" she howled. "Do you think he was murdered?"

"We must look at all possibilities."

"Oh man," she laughed. "Don't waste your time. I'll tell you what happened. He went out to watch the sunset like he always does, had too much to drink like he always does, and fell into the pool." She shrugged. "He can't swim."

CHAPTER 5

Darcy knocked softly on Meredith's door. Getting no answer, she slowly turned the nob and pushed the door open just enough to stick her head in. "May I come in?"

Meredith was sitting at her desk with her head in her hands. Her earlier gaiety now replaced with despondency. The letter was on the desk in front of her. Darcy could see the carefully cut out magazine words and letters glued to it. Same as last time. "You okay?" she asked.

Meredith invited her in with the wave of her hand. She looked up, her beautiful gray eyes full of turmoil. "How could this be?"

Darcy could hear the fear in Meredith's voice. "I'm so sorry," she said in consolation.

"I just can't believe it. This wasn't how it was supposed to go. I thought we were done with this. I already paid that weasel. How could this be?" she cried.

"I'm so sorry," Darcy repeated as she took a seat in the chair across from her. "You should just stop this affair and put an end to it," she said firmly.

Meredith wasn't listening to her. "I know it was Art, that monster. I mean who else could it possibly be? Who else would know? He's always been taking advantage of us. Pretending to protect Dirk – that's all a bunch of hogwash. He'd like nothing better than to humiliate him."

Darcy leaned forward across the desk to get Meredith's attention. "When are you going to quit seeing this guy so all this can stop?"

Meredith rubbed her forehead. "Well, I will, once…"

"Once what?" Darcy demanded.

Meredith closed her eyes. "Once I'm ready, that's all. I just don't know yet."

"You don't know yet?" Darcy exclaimed.

Meredith shook her head. "No," she sighed. "I don't know yet." Meredith knew Darcy had just been doing her job collecting and sorting the mail that day when the first one arrived, but how she wished Darcy had never seen that letter. Now Meredith had to deal with both the black-mailer's demands *and* Darcy's berating. "Please, please, please just forget about that, will you? That doesn't matter." She picked up the letter and shook it in the air. "How did this get here?" She stood and started pacing.

"It was in the mail slot – just like the other one. I knew what it was, so I thought it best to put it on your desk so no one else would see it."

Meredith stopped pacing and put her hands on her hips. "Art must have put it there last night. Did you see it there when you left?"

"I didn't check the mail last night."

"No, of course you didn't." Meredith continued pacing. "That sneaky snake," she said. "He knew you wouldn't check the mail."

"Right," Darcy nodded. "It could have been there last night. But you know Meredith, anyone could have dropped it in the box last night. Can I see it?"

"Sure." She dropped the letter on the desk in front of Darcy.

Darcy looked at the words pasted on the page, each in a different font, from different articles and advertisements. It looked like an eerie piece of art. It said:

Deliver Fifty Thousand $$ to bus stop
5th & Washington
put in trash can tomorrow @ 8 am
or else DIRK will get photos

"Dirk" was spelled out in all capital letters, each letter cut out individually. Darcy handed the letter back to Meredith. "I'm sorry, Meredith," she said again. "Fifty thousand? Can you get another fifty thousand?"

Meredith walked over and plopped back down in her chair. "Yes." She shrugged. "It's really just Art's money anyway."

Darcy sat back in her seat and let out a long sigh.

"The money's not the problem," Meredith said. She looked up at Darcy. "The photos are still out there. I need to find the photos."

"Why not just let it go? Stop this affair. The pictures would be worthless."

"No," Meredith said. "You don't understand. If Dirk saw them…" she let the sentence trail off. She wrung her hands together. She knew she should tell him. She had promised that she would. She heaved a deep sigh. "I should just tell him," she said aloud.

"Meredith," Darcy said. "Don't be daft. You don't need to tell Dirk, you just need to stop seeing this other guy."

Meredith buried her head in her hands. "But I'm just not ready to yet…. It's just not the time…. I need more time." She jumped up from her desk. "I'm going to find them."

"Find them? The pictures? Meredith, they're in the Cloud. They're just out there floating around somewhere."

"I'm going down there," Meredith declared as she walked to the filing cabinet. She pulled open the middle drawer and started feeling underneath.

"What are you doing?"

"Got it." Meredith peeled off the key that was taped to the bottom that opened the door to Art's basement studio. "I should have done this the first time."

"But why? There's nothing to find."

"You don't know that." She shook a finger at Darcy. "Don't tell anyone about this."

"What if Art comes in and finds you down there?'

"Like you said, he's probably sleeping off a hangover," Meredith said as she headed toward the door. But then she stopped dead in her tracks and put her hand to her cheek. "But still – just in case – would you please watch out the front windows for me? Keep the door locked. If you see anyone coming, call me."

"Okay."

"Shred that horrible letter then get out front," she directed as she crossed the gallery to the basement door. "And please remember to move those easels back from the windows!"

♦ ♦ ♦

Meredith unlocked the door, flipped on the light switch and stepped down the stairs to the basement level –

Artimus' lair. While most artists preferred to work in well-lit rooms, Art preferred the dark.

She'd only been there once before. It was several years ago, not long after Dirk's parents purchased the building for the sole purpose of allowing Art to display and sell his paintings as their heartfelt thanks to Art for saving the life of their beloved son. Art had commandeered the entire lower level for himself, and Dirk and Meredith suspected that he intended to live there, since they didn't think he had anywhere else to go.

In the beginning, and because of the insistence of his parents, Dirk tried to run the gallery. But after he could no longer stomach the sight of Art, Meredith stepped in to take charge. And it was completely unimaginable then, what a huge success this little gallery would become.

Upstairs, Darcy pulled the easels well back from the windows as instructed, then took a seat on one of the pedestals that contained a sculpture entitled "World Peace." She didn't get it. In her opinion, it just looked like a bunch of old metal pieces welded together in no particular form. But the best part about this specific piece, was that there was plenty of room on the pedestal for her to sit and watch out front, while also being partially hidden by one of the easels she had just moved. She looked around the gallery at all the sculptures, paintings, carvings and a variety of art made from recycled materials like the sculpture next to her. She just couldn't believe she was actually working at this gallery – and was even more amazed that she was working so closely with Meredith Stanton.

◆ ◆ ◆

If her boyfriend hadn't come to Minneapolis, Darcy knew she wouldn't be here in the position she was in. She wouldn't be in Minneapolis at all. He was the reason for all she did. It had taken some careful planning to get here, but surprisingly enough, things had worked out even better than she had hoped.

She remembered when she passed by the gallery just over four months ago and noticed the 'Help Wanted' sign in the window. She remembered going back to her room and spending hours crafting her resume to give her the very best odds of getting hired. She remembered showing up at the gallery door the very next day and requesting an interview. She remembered being shocked to learn that it would be Meredith, herself, conducting the interview. And she couldn't help but laugh out loud remembering the crazy, totally mind-boggling conversation that had followed.

◆ ◆ ◆

Meredith had been quite impressed with Darcy's resume showing prior positions in well-known New York Galleries, and had asked the usual perfunctory questions.

How did you hear about this position? Tell me about yourself. Tell me about your past job history. What were your duties? How do you handle stress? Tell me about a conflict you faced at work and how you dealt with it. Why do you want this position?

And Darcy had handled them all with aplomb.

But then the interview took an unexpected turn.

"One of our resident artists is quite crude," Meredith told her. "Are you easily offended by off-color jokes?"

"What?" Darcy responded, a bit blindsided.

Meredith's grey eyes searched Darcy's face. "Can you handle yourself if he comes on to you?"

Darcy shifted in her seat. "I – I suppose so."

"Because he comes on to everyone," Meredith explained. She shook her head in disgust. "You would need to expect this."

Darcy pushed the bangs back from her forehead. "Oh. Ah, okay," she responded.

"You'd need to speak up for yourself and put him in his place." Meredith locked eyes with Darcy. "*Aggressively*," she added.

Darcy nodded slowly. "Okay," she replied.

"Slapping is encouraged," Meredith said. She leaned forward, eyebrows raised. "Are you able to do that?"

Darcy almost let out a hoot at the absurdity of it all, then reeled it in. "Hey, no problem. I grew up with four brothers," she lied. "I can do that."

"Good." Meredith smiled. "Would you sign a release to that effect?

Darcy shrugged. "Um, sure."

"Excellent." Meredith extended her hand across her desk.

Darcy was hired on the spot. And that was her introduction to the world-renowned Artimus.

♦♦♦

Darcy heard the squeal of the brakes as the Fox 9 van parked outside, pulling her back to the here and now. The occupants jumped out and headed her way. Then another TV van pulled in just behind. Darcy quickly slid off the pedestal and high-tailed it to the back of the gallery.

"Meredith!" she called, just as Meredith pushed through the basement door knocking Darcy to the floor.

"There are news reporters out front!" Darcy announced from below.

Meredith gasped. "News reporters are here? Already?"

Darcy scrambled to her feet and pointed toward the front. "Just outside."

Meredith leaned over for a look. Sure enough, news crews were beginning to set up outside. "Wow. That was fast."

They heard knocking at the door.

"Why are they here?" Darcy asked.

Meredith turned and shut the door to the basement. "I just had a call from Dirk. He says we must not open the gallery today."

"But why not? What's going on?"

Meredith took her by the shoulders. "Art is dead."

Darcy stiffened, her eyes wide. "Dead?"

"The news reports say he drowned in his pool last night."

"Drowned in his pool? That's what they say?"

"Yes," Meredith replied. She took another peek around the corner. "What a terrible accident. You'd think he would have learned how to swim by now."

"Right," Darcy agreed. "A terrible accident."

CHAPTER 6

Isaac slipped the key fob back in his pocket, pushed through the garage door of his home, and was practically tackled by Walter, their mixed breed, sixty-pound, one-year-old knucklehead of a dog who always greeted Isaac with overflowing enthusiasm. Isaac sighed. It didn't appear the obedience training was working.

"Down!" Isaac commanded.

Walter dropped down and started circling Isaac, sniffing him all over, up and down.

"Stop it, Walter. SIT," Isaac commanded.

Walter dutifully sat, but his nose continued to take in the unpleasant aroma emanating from Isaac.

Isaac had been surveying the scene outside by Artimus' pool and the perimeter of the premises in the heat. His clothing was damp from perspiration and stuck to his body in the most personal of spots. If you didn't know better, you might think he had taken a swim fully dressed.

Why was it that dogs were drawn to stinky things, Isaac wondered. "Walter, that is so impolite," he said.

Walter wagged his tail happily in response.

Isaac heard the familiar pitter patter of rubber soled shoes.

"Heavens to Betsy! What's all the commotion going on out here?" Edna said as she came around the corner.

"Hi Edna. It's just me and the knucklehead."

Walter wagged his tail again.

"My word, Detective," she exclaimed at the site of him. "You don't look so good. Why don't you come over here and sit a spell?"

Edna was the family's nanny, cleaning lady, and more importantly, their dear friend. Isaac met Edna when he was investigating the death of her prior employer. Edna had called him "Detective" then, and, despite the change in their relationship, still called him that.

Isaac's son, Jacob, the family comedian, decided it would be fun to start using this moniker as well. So, from the ten-year-old's mouth Isaac would hear, "Would you hand me the remote, Detective? Hey Detective, wanna shoot some hoops?" and the like."

But while Jacob thought this was hilarious, it made Isaac's oldest daughter, Avery, incensed. It seemed her father's occupation was interfering with her dating status and the ability to make love connections. The boys at her school didn't want to date the daughter of a cop.

Isaac didn't mind this a bit. He knew all too well what was on the minds of teenage boys having been one himself. The way Isaac figured, it was quite fortunate that all those potential young suitors were aware of his occupation. This made the odds far more likely that only an upstanding gentleman would be courting his daughter.

Still, Isaac wasn't keen on the idea of having his own son call him anything but "Dad." After all, there were only three people in the world that could call him that. And other than his wife, Claudia, they were the three people he cared about most in the world. His children. His pride and joy. When he would point this out to Jacob, Jacob would roll his eyes and say something like "Okay, Detective Dad." or "If you say so, Detective Dad." It was not exactly the result Isaac had hoped for, but he figured it was a good compromise.

After all, he knew this was due to Edna's influence. In her folksy way, she was quick to endear herself to all. He knew that he could ask his children to do something until he was blue in the face, but if Edna asked them to do it, the kids listened — and actually did it. The kids told Edna things they didn't feel comfortable talking with their parents about. She was their sounding board. And he knew the advice and counsel she gave them would be sound. He was exceedingly grateful she had come into his life – into all of their lives. Edna was indeed a true blessing.

"Thanks, Edna, but what I really need right now is a shower and a change of clothing," Isaac responded.

"Tsk, tsk." She clucked. "Have you been outside in this heat, Detective?" She eyed his waistline. "In the shape you're in? You've got a few too many pounds around that mid-section, you know."

He winked at her. "All thanks to your cooking, Edna."

"Just the same, that's no place for man nor beast today. It's a wonder you didn't keel right on over and end up in a hospital bed. I thought you knew better 'n that."

"Believe me, Edna. It couldn't be helped."

"Oh, for goodness' sake, you poor thing. Let me get you a tall, cold glass of water." She scrambled over to the sink. "And Heaven help us, my warnings didn't stop those children of yours from running out back either." She pulled a glass from the cupboard. "Payin' no mind to the sense God gave 'em, I tell you." She pushed the glass into the refrigerator faucet. "Now don't you move a muscle," she said. "Ice-cold water coming right up!"

Isaac leaned over and pet Walter on the head. "Thanks, Edna."

Edna bustled over and handed him the water. Her bright eyes twinkled. "I'll whip you up a good lunch while you get yourself cleaned up and cooled down."

It was amazing to him how much energy was packed into this barely five-foot package. At seventy-six years old she could run circles around most people twenty years younger. He took a long drink. "That sounds wonderful. Thanks, Edna."

Just then, his five-year-old, Isabelle, burst through the back door. "Edna!" she cried. "There's a demon duck in the pond!"

"There's a what?" Isaac asked.

Isabelle whirled around to see her father was unexpectedly home. Her eyes grew wide. "Daddy, Daddy! There's a demon duck in the pond! It's really big and has red eyes!"

"A demon duck?"

"Yes, yes," she confirmed, her head bobbing. She grabbed his hand, pulling him toward the door. "Come see!"

They stepped out the door to find Jacob with a big grin on his face. "Oh, um, hi, Detective. We weren't expecting you to be home today."

"I'll bet you weren't – and it's "Dad" to you." Isaac shook his finger at him. "Jacob, what tall tale have you been telling your little sister this time?"

"No daddy, it's REAL" Isabelle insisted. "I saw it! Come see!"

Jacob just smiled and shrugged.

Just then an eerie call came from the pond. They all stopped to listen. Isaac could see Isabelle's mouth drop open and shivers run up her little spine.

Isaac recognized the call immediately. "Come here, honey." He picked her up and gave Jacob the evil eye. "That call comes from a Loon. It's a big black and white sort of duck with red eyes." He started toward the pond. "Who called it a demon duck?"

"Jacob did. He said it would peck all the other ducks to death."

"He did, did he?"

Jacob shrugged again. "It sure looked like it would. It was charging at the Mallards and causing a big ruckus. Pretty cool."

"Can you put me down, Daddy?" Isabelle asked. She crinkled her little nose. "You're kinda wet and stinky."

Isaac chuckled and set her down. One could always depend on the honesty of a five-year-old.

They reached the park, and sure enough, there was a Loon. It was a small pond, so it was not a good place for a loon to be. The Loon flapped its wings and wailed. Isabelle jumped behind her father. "It's scary, Daddy."

"No honey, I think maybe *it's* scared."

"Why would it be scared, Daddy?"

"Well honey, you see how big it is?" It was twice the size of the other ducks in the pond.

She nodded.

"It needs a long stretch of water to get it's big body into the air, and this pond is pretty small."

Isabelle inched out from behind Isaac's legs.

"I think it's scared that it can't leave."

The Loon reared up and charged at a Mallard that was getting a little too close, flapping its broad wings and yodeling loudly, causing Isabelle to jump back behind Isaac's legs. "It's scary, Daddy."

"It's cool," Jacob said. "It has red eyes."

♦♦♦

Back home, Isaac showered up and when he came downstairs, he found the kids eating their lunch in front of the TV watching a documentary about Loons which he was sure Edna found for them.

"Now you go on and take a seat right over there, Detective," Edna directed. "I've got some chicken salad for you."

Isaac looked at his watch, then at the chicken salad Edna had prepared. Edna's chicken salad was undeniably the best chicken salad in the world. That being the case, he decided it would be okay if he was a few minutes late to his meeting. Vick was routinely late, and Isaac doubted that propensity had righted itself during Vick's time in California. "Thanks, Edna," he said. "It looks delicious. Why don't you join me?"

"Don't mind if I do." Edna dropped a dollop of the chicken salad onto a plate and took the seat across from him. "So, I hear there's a Loon in the pond."

"Yes. Why it decided to land there, I just don't know. It makes me wonder if it's wounded or something. I'll call Animal Control about it."

"Oh pooh," she said. "I can take care of that." She reached over and pat his hand. "You go get some rest now. This family depends on you. You need to take care of yourself."

"A rest sounds good, Edna, but I'm afraid I've got to get to a meeting this afternoon."

"Poppy cock," she said. "What's so all-fired important that you can't just handle it from here?" She set her fork down and placed both of her hands flat on the table. "I don't think you should be going back out in this heat. You don't want to get heat stroke, you know."

Isaac smiled and took her tiny, wrinkled hand, clasping it between his. "Don't you worry, Edna," he said. "I'll have air conditioning all the way." Then he gave her a curious look. "Have you ever heard of Artimus?"

"Artimus? Sure have."

"You have?" Isaac responded, unable to keep the surprise from his voice.

"Sure thing. He donated a painting for Crystal's Palace."

"He did?" Artimus, the Van Gogh of Minnesota, donated a painting to a home for the families of cancer victims?

"Yep. Hangs right there in the reception room. One of the first things the patient and their family see when being admitted."

"Did you meet him?" Isaac asked, since besides being the family's nanny, housekeeper and dear friend, Edna was the one who funded the building of Crystal's Palace with the inheritance she received after her former employer, was murdered. But that was another story.

"Nope. But that good deed added Mr. Artimus to my prayer chain," Edna pronounced. "It's signed and everything. Not sure what it's supposed to be, but the colors are nice. Kind of a swirly thing. Like what my kids used to finger paint."

CHAPTER 7

Darcy's shoes clicked against the tile floor as she hustled across the gallery to the front door. Seeing her, the reporters rushed in shouting questions, microphones in hand, cameras at the ready, their bodies and faces right up against the glass.

"Is it true Artimus is dead?"

"Did Artimus drown in his pool?"

"Was there foul play?"

It was an unsettling sight. Her hands shook as she taped the typewritten notice Dirk had dictated setting forth the gallery's official statement honoring the great Artimus and giving notice that the gallery would be closed for mourning the next week, right over one of the reporter's faces.

The hope was that once the reporters saw it, they would respectfully move on. But they didn't.

"Was he alone in the house?"

"Will his death affect the value of his paintings?"

"Was this a crime of passion?"

Darcy gave them as sad a look as she could muster and pointed at the sign, but it only made them more insistent. Art's death had understandably created quite a stir, but there was no way she was ever going to open that door. Couldn't they read?

She backed away a few steps, waved at them, then turned and quickly went back to her office.

When she started this job she could never have anticipated this turn of events. But then again, she never anticipated getting this job in the first place. Funny how life can teeter-totter like that. Certainly, there was no question that Art's death would change things.

She poured herself a cup of coffee and started making calls to the staff. As expected, the news produced the commensurate reactions of shock and titillation over the nature of Artimus' death from all. But despite their words of grief and acclamations of his work, it was plain Artimus was not well liked — particularly with the female members of the staff. He was a lecher of the worst kind.

Remembering the day she actually met Art in person made her skin crawl. It had been her second official day on the job.

♦ ♦ ♦

Art had lumbered by her office, then stopped abruptly and leaned back, peering through the door. "Well, hel-loow," he said to her, drawing out the "o" sound at the end of the word.

"Hello to you," she responded, not knowing who he was.

He stepped into the office.

"How can I help you?" Darcy asked.

He grinned. "I think it might be me who can help you, darlin'."

"Oh?"

"Oh, yes," he said. He twirled his meaty pointer finger at her. "Now just who are you, sweetcakes?"

Sweetcakes? She hated him immediately but stood and extended her hand. "I'm Darcy, Meredith Stanton's assistant."

"The woman does deliver," he said with a smile. He stepped up to Darcy's desk and took her extended hand, kissing the top. "I'm the great Artimus."

"Oh my," she said as she pulled her hand away and wiped it on her slacks. Never in a million years would she have guessed that. "I'm so honored to meet you. I love your work."

"Of course you do. Everyone does. We should get together and talk about it over drinks." He winked at her. "My place?"

"Oh, I don't think…"

"No need to think, you little minx. You should stop by tonight. I just got the pool filled."

"Ha!" she scoffed. "It's April. Isn't it a bit chilly for swimming?"

"Babe," he leaned across the desk. "I'm sure between you and me, we could make it so hot, the pool would turn into a Jacuzzi."

She leered at him. Meredith hadn't been kidding. Her fingers twitched as she readied herself to slap him.

"I'll bet you look great in a bikini."

"Well, no I - "

"Don't' be shy," he interrupted. "Sure you do." He reached over and pulled her blouse away from her chest.

She grabbed the fabric back and held it tight when, thankfully, Meredith emerged from her office.

"Art. It's you," Meredith said. "What are you doing here?"

"Just meeting your new assistant, Doll." He looked over at Darcy and licked his lips. "Nice choice."

"Get out of here and leave her alone, Art."

"Whatever you say, Doll." He turned and blew Darcy a kiss. "Bye, bye, darlin'."

"Her name's Darcy!" Meredith shouted after him.

That was certainly not the end of it, and Darcy did have to slap him once or twice after that to make him move on. But he never stopped coming at her. He was relentless.

♦♦♦

Meredith had spent the last half hour down below trying to figure out how to artfully get Darcy out of the office. Darcy may unfortunately be privy to the blackmailing, but Meredith could not, would not, let Darcy find out about what she had just discovered in Art's lair.

Meredith climbed the stairs and stood on the top step, her hand on the door handle. She took a deep breath to calm herself, then took another, then turned the handle and stepped through the door.

She peered around the corner at the front windows. It looked as if the press had departed, thank goodness. She walked through the gallery and found Darcy at her desk.

Darcy looked up at her expectantly. "Did you find anything down there?"

Meredith shook her head. "No," she lied, knowing that it was certain she would never tell a soul what she *did* find. Not even Dirk. If word ever got out about it, the value of Artimus' paintings would plummet. That scoundrel! All in all, she had to admit that she wasn't surprised by it. They were dealing with Artie Farkus, after all. The biggest bullshitter that walked the earth.

"Meredith, did you really think you'd find actual photos? And even if you did, more can always be printed. They're in the cloud," Darcy said.

"Right. That's right. I don't know what I was thinking, but…." Meredith rubbed the back of her neck. "When you're right, you're right." She clasped her hands together. "Well, it looks like the press has thankfully moved on, so you can get going now," she told Darcy.

Darcy sat back in her seat. "Are you sure?"

"Yes, yes. As long as everyone has been notified that we're closed, there's no need for you to hang around."

"They've been notified," Darcy confirmed. "They didn't seem too broken up by the news," she added wryly.

"I'm not surprised. Art was a pariah." Meredith had always said it and now she had the proof. "But." She leaned back against the office wall and held her pointer finger in the air. "There's one good thing that comes out of Art's death." She smiled. "I won't need to pay another ransom."

Darcy gasped. "You're not going to pay it? But what if Art wasn't the blackmailer? Are you ready to take that chance?"

Meredith threw up her hands in exasperation. "Geez, Darcy. Who else could it be?"

"I don't know. I mean, what do you really know about this guy you're hooking up with?" Darcy raised her eyebrows. "Maybe he's screwing you in more ways than one."

"Darcy! How rude!"

"I'm sorry. I didn't mean to hurt *you*. I'm just wondering about HIS character. Would he be the sort to take advantage of you?"

"Oh no. He wouldn't. We have an understanding."

"An understanding?" She rolled her eyes. "How romantic."

"Please just stop it, would you? It's not like that. I'm sure it's not him, okay?"

"Okay. Okay." She held up her hands in surrender. "But seriously, Meredith. It could be anyone, really. Anyone who knows you and Dirk — and wants your money. You're a well-known person around here. There are all sorts of people who would take advantage of a situation like this."

"Darcy, I never knew you were so mistrusting."

"Look, I'm just being prudent. If you *don't* drop the money, and the blackmailer wasn't Art, you'll have a lot of explaining to do to your dearest love." She used air quotes around the words "dearest love."

"Ugh!" Meredith exclaimed and started pacing. She really didn't need this right now. But maybe Darcy had a point. On the other hand, she had been so sure Art was the culprit. How would anyone else know? She placed her hands on her hips. "It *had* to be Art," she said aloud.

"Really Meredith?" Darcy leaned back in her seat, eyebrows raised. "I'm going to ask you again. Are you willing to take that chance?"

Meredith pulled the stray flaxen hairs back from her forehead. "I don't know." She turned and started back the other direction. "If Dirk ever saw those pictures, he'd be so hurt." She twisted the wedding ring on her finger. "I need to tell him. I know I need to tell him." She shoved her hands in her pockets. "But now with Art dead and all that Dirk is dealing with because of that, it just doesn't seem like the right time…."

"Well then, don't you think you should drop the money as instructed? If Art was your blackmailer, the money will still be there where you left it and you could go collect it."

Meredith stopped her pacing. "But somebody else could take it."

"Yes, I suppose that's the risk you'd have to take. Even so, if you don't get another blackmail letter, you'd know the blackmailer was indeed Art." She raised her brows. "Either way, you're safer in the long run. Isn't that worth it?"

"I suppose you're right," Meredith grumbled. It had seemed so obvious to her that Art was the culprit, but she now had to admit it could be another. "Shit." She dropped into her chair. Most importantly, she needed to protect Dirk. The wheels started turning in her head. She raised her pointer finger to the air. "How about if this time you pretend you're me and make the drop? Then I can watch to see if anyone shows up to collect it."

"You want me to pretend to be you?"

"Yes."

"That's just plain crazy," Darcy said. They were about the same height, but that's where the resemblance ended.

"Please?"

Darcy grunted. "Meredith, I don't know if you've noticed, but I have brown hair." She tugged on few strands. "And it's short," she added.

"You can wear one of my floppy hats."

"Your floppy hat?" Darcy stood and swooshed her hands from head to toe. "But what about the rest of me, Meredith? I doubt anyone would mistake me for you in any number of ways."

Meredith shrugged. "I'll bring my big raincoat."

Darcy threw her arms up to the sky. "But it's not expected to rain!"

"You don't know that."

"Yes. I do. I look at the weather forecast. It's going to be hot and sunny tomorrow. Just like today."

Meredith stomped her foot on the floor. "Stop it, will you? You're the one who wants me to do this." Enough was enough. "It will be fine."

Darcy shut her lips tightly.

Meredith took a deep breath. "I'll take your car and park nearby. Then you can drive my car. From a distance no one will know you aren't me."

"I'm not so sure about that," Darcy said doubtfully. "But if that's the way you want it, I'll do it." She pointed a finger at Meredith. "Bring that raincoat."

CHAPTER 8

"Hey Peg," Isaac called as he entered the station.

"Arrggh!" she exclaimed, fists to the sky.

"Whoa," Isaac said. "You okay?" Peg was the assistant and point person for all the detectives at the station. If you wanted to know anything about anything at the office, Peg was your gal. She'd been there as long as he could remember. But he couldn't ever remember seeing her like this.

"The phone has been ringing nonstop with calls from all sorts of news agencies about the drowning of Artimus.

Who is this Artimus, anyway?" she squawked. "Have you ever heard of him?

But before he could answer, another call came in.

She pointed at the screen. "See?" she cried. "Humpf! It's Mimi Winslow again. She's called at least a dozen times." Peg sat back and crossed her arms over her chest. "I'm not answering."

Isaac leaned against the counter above her desk. "She's probably mad because I scared her with my siren," he said.

Peg looked up at him and smirked. "What's that you say?" She sat forward in her seat. "Ha! Tell me. Tell me."

"Well," Isaac began. "I was trying to get down the street to the scene, and she was right there in the middle of the road. I tried several times to gently urge her to move."

"Gently?" she asked skeptically.

"Yes, *very* gently. The lights were flashing, I tapped my horn, I moved in closer. Everyone else had cleared the way, but she wouldn't go. So," he shrugged. "I used my siren." The corners of his mouth rose. "And it scared her right out of her stilettos."

"You didn't." She shook her finger at him. "You rascal."

"Yep. Poor thing. She ended up on her behind on the hot pavement right in the middle of the street. You should have seen her scramble off."

Peg grinned wide showing the little gap between her two front teeth. "That's the best thing I've heard all day.

I hope some quick-thinking camera man got footage of it. I'd love to see *that* on the news!" She opened her desk drawer, pulled out a file and handed it to Isaac. "I'll bet you're here for this," she said. "F-Y-I, Captain Petruco is running late. Like me, he's also been busy with all the media people. But the difference is, he's loving it." She drew out the "l" sound in the word 'loving' to emphasize just how much he was indeed loving it. "For him, this is a dream come true!"

It was so. Petuco liked nothing better than being in front of a crowd – particularly a nationwide crowd. And he was good at it. He was a showman. It was certain that was the reason he held his job. On the other hand, he was not a very good leader. But, over their years together, Isaac had been able to figure out ways to take the lead and make Petruco feel like he was still in charge. Mostly, it worked.

"Vick's here, though," Peg added with a twinkle in her eyes.

"Vick's here?" Isaac said with astonishment. "On time?"

"Yeah, isn't it great he's back?"

Peg had always had a crush on handsome Vick. "Peg, shame on you, you're a happily married woman."

"Oh, so true. Isaac. But that doesn't mean I can't look."

◆◆◆

Isaac pushed through the meeting room door. "Vick?" he exclaimed. "Is that really you? On time for a meeting?" He dropped the file on the table. "Maybe California *did* do you some good."

"Hey, hey, hey," Vick responded. "I've got a date tonight and don't want to be bogged down with all of this all afternoon."

"Bogged down with all of this?" Isaac repeated, realizing nothing had changed. "Well, I sure hope this investigation won't interfere with your social life."

"No shit. Petruco is all fired up about this one. He's going to be all over us to figure this out as quickly as possible. But." He raised his forefinger. "Fortunately, I think we already know the answer."

"We do?"

"Yeah, it's like Sis said. Her brother likes to drink by the pool and fell in." He shrugged. "I don't know, maybe he tripped over that lawn chair and they both ended up in the pool. Sis says he can't swim. So he just drown. No foul play. Just an accident."

"Maybe." Isaac pondered that scenario. A crease appeared on Isaac's forehead. "Why would he have a pool if he can't swim in it? Are we sure that's correct?"

Vick sat back in his seat. "Oh, I got the answer to that one too. Sis said he had the pool because he liked to see his dates in wet bikinis." Vick smiled. "Sounds like a pretty good reason to me."

Isaac sighed. "Oh, Vick." He pulled out a chair and reached for the folder. "So what did you see in the file?"

"I haven't had a chance to look yet - had to catch up on my texts."

"Well, Mr. Popular, it's time to put the phone away. Let's go through it together."

Vick put his cell phone in his pocket. "Okay, Magnificent One, use those awesome instincts of yours and let's get this wrapped up."

They both opened their folders and began to read through the evidence.

"Holy shit!" Vick exclaimed. "This guy was hiding his money all over the house! They found millions!"

It was true. They found stacks of money in kitchen tins, under the mattress, taped to the bottoms of drawers, in the attic, and inside books where the pages had been cut out to accommodate large stacks of hundred-dollar bills, just to name a few. It was like in the depression era – except a millionfold.

"I guess he didn't trust banks," Isaac observed wryly.

The other things that were plentiful throughout the house were porn magazines and liquor.

"I think the discovery of the magazines helps support Sis's answer to why big bro has a pool," Vick declared. "Don't you? It's quite a collection. Going back fifteen years." Vick got a mischievous look on his face. "You know Isaac, I think I should examine those further. See if

Artie might have left any notes in them or something that might lead us to his killer."

Isaac shook his head. When would men ever grow up and stop viewing woman as mindless objects, he wondered? On the other hand, he knew his brilliant wife, Claudia, would wonder when women would grow up and stop *letting* men view them as mindless objects. At any rate, if it did turn out that this was a murder investigation, they most likely *would* need to go through those magazines, and Isaac was happy not to be the one to do it. "Well, if this turns out to be a murder investigation, they're all yours."

"Oh yeah." Vick ran his hands over his slick hair. "My pleasure."

"Hey wait a minute," Isaac said. "I thought you had determined this was an accidental drowning."

"Oh sure, of course. But I think we'll have some time before we have confirmation of that from Cynthia, so I'll get right on the review of those magazines – just in case."

Petruco burst through the door interrupting their discussion. He was a swarthy man with a large beak and hunched shoulders. His beady eyes moved back and forth between them like a vulture after prey. "Where's Bryant?" he asked.

"He's on vacation, Captain," Isaac responded.

"But I'm back, and better than ever," Vick announced.

Petruco walked into the room to the head of the table. "Good. Good. This is a big one. World renowned, highly acclaimed and highly honored, Artimus." Petruco bent his head in honor of the man. "A Minnesota treasure has been lost."

"Did you know him, Captain?" Isaac asked.

"Ah, no." He clapped his hands, then rubbed them together. "But I sure do now." He took a seat and leaned forward on his elbows. "So, what do you think? Was this murder? Suicide? Accident? I need to know," he said impatiently. "The press are hounding me. I have no privacy. They're everywhere. This man was known world-wide," he said. "Who knew?"

Isaac knew full well that all Petruco's complaining about being hounded by the press was just bluster, and he could see that Petruco was having trouble keeping the smile from his face. "Nothing at the crime scene is giving us clues as to how Artimus drown," Isaac told him. "We're waiting for the results of the autopsy. Cynthia Chu is the medical examiner working on this case and she's the best we have, so I feel confident that she will be able to get us a more concrete assessment of what happened."

Petruco drummed his fingertips on the table. "Cynthia Chu, huh? When can we expect the results?"

"I guess it depends on what she finds. Hopefully it was accidental, but until we hear otherwise, we'll continue interviewing those that knew him to try to get a sense of what was happening in his life, and to see if he had any enemies or thoughts of suicide."

"What did you find at the scene?" Petruco asked.

"Not much, sorry to say," Isaac responded. He picked up the file. "No signs of an altercation, except maybe the lawn chair in the pool. It's a little bent up, but it's hard to say when those dents happened. The forensics team is looking at it. The house was cleaned immediately prior to finding the victim, so we didn't find any fingerprints - other than those of the sister who was the one who cleaned the house. It says here that the forensics team is checking a few fibers and strands of hair they found in the carpeting and residue of something on the guest towel in the main bath. Lots of glitter everywhere."

"Glitter?" Petruco asked, intrigued.

"Yes, but we believe that came from the sister's clothing," Isaac explained. "No blood stains were found." He flipped the page. "Mr. Farkus had some odd habits like hiding cash all over his house."

"Yeah, if this was a robbery, the robbers missed a fortune," Vick chimed in.

"We'll check to see if he had any bank accounts anywhere," Isaac said. "He was in the army when he was younger and was awarded a medal of honor."

"Impressive," Petruco declared.

"Yes," Isaac agreed. He set the report back on the table. "There's a lot more to go through in here, Captain. So that's just a summary of what we've got so far."

"And don't forget this," Vick said. "The great Artimus had an extensive collection of porn magazines - which

I have selflessly offered to search if there turns out to be foul play."

"Ha!" Petruco exclaimed and gave Vick a high five. "Good man! Let me know if you need any assistance with that."

CHAPTER 9

The fan blew the hot air around the efficiency apartment as Fiona pulled the suitcase out from under her bed, threw open her closet doors and made quick work of packing her creations. She added some personal items, her mother's photo album and a few other nick-nacks.

That should do it, she thought to herself. The rest of her belongings were all replaceable. She set the suitcase by the door, went to the bathroom and doused a washcloth with cold water. She set it on her face, then draped it across the back of her neck letting the water drip down her burning skin. She smiled at herself in the mirror. This was it. Her new life had just begun. The spotlight would be hers now.

She sat at her desk, pulled a pad of Post-It notes from the drawer and scribbled "Here's my ninety-day notice and last three months' rent" on the top one. She opened her satchel, counted out three months' rent, removed the apartment key from her key chain, then shoved it, the rent money and the note inside an envelope. She pulled down the duffle bag full of Art's money from the top shelf of the closet. With suitcase and duffle bag in hand, she went down to the caretaker's apartment and slipped the envelope under the door. "Good riddance to this apartment and good riddance to Art," she said aloud as she stepped out the door with her belongings.

◆◆◆

Fiona parked in the lot across the street from the hotel and took a look in the mirror to be sure she didn't have any mascara melting down her face. The police wouldn't let her take Art's Ferrari yet, so she was still driving the beat-up Chevy with the broken air conditioning system. She grinned as she got out of the car and crossed the street to the hotel. She would never, ever have to go back to that steam room of an apartment. The miserable part of the day was past her. Welcome to wonderful!

She walked into the lobby and was immediately confronted with one of her brother's "paintings." She always thought it proper to use air quotes around that word when describing her brother's artwork because she knew the truth about them. In fact, it had been her idea in the beginning. She stopped and looked at it. It was an original. Not bad. He was almost able to stay inside the lines.

"May I help you?" came a voice from behind her.

Fiona turned to find a handsome looking woman with tightly clasped hands, a forced sort-of smile, and eyes that said go away. Her nametag said her name was Patience.

"Yes," Fiona replied. "I'd like a room. A suite."

Patience pursed her lips. This girl looked nothing like their usual clientele. "Our suites run over two hundred dollars a night. Are you sure you wouldn't be happier at a Super 8?"

Fiona sneered at her, dropped her satchel on the floor, pulled out a wad of cash and fanned it through her fingers. "Two hundred dollars a night is a drop in the bucket for me," she replied with a large, snarky smile. At least it will be once she had her inheritance, she thought to herself.

Patience wrung her hands as the possible reasons someone like this girl would have a bag full of cash bounced around inside her head. Was it stolen? Drug money? Could she be some kind of rock star? Should she call the police?

Fiona watched Patience fidget. How she loved to make people squirm. But, she reminded herself, that would need to change now. She quickly wiped the smirk from her face. The new Fiona wanted people to like her, so much so that they wanted to *look* like her, and would want to buy her clothing creations. "And I know your hotel accommodations are worth every penny," she said as kindly as she could muster.

"Let me check with the manager," Patience finally said, then hustled toward the offices.

"Very good. Oh, and I'd like a room with a view of the lake," Fiona called after her. "Please," she added as an afterthought. It was a good thing her aunt had given her some instruction in manners, because she sure hadn't had instruction like that from Artie. All these years of having to put up with his abuse were finally going to pay off. Art was now an asset to her. *Imagine that!*

Patience and a tall man with a spray-on tan arrived momentarily. "Excuse me, miss," he said.

But before he could say any more, Fiona turned away from the painting and held out her hand. "Hello. Let me introduce myself, I'm Fiona Farkus, sister of Artimus Farkus. It's so lovely to see you have one of his paintings in your lobby – and an original at that. I knew I chose the right place to stay during this terrible time."

The manager and woman exchanged glances. Could this be so? The great Artimus had a sister?

"Miss Farkus, it's very nice to meet you," the man told her, while inside wondering if this was all a scam. He reached out and took her hand. "I'm Duncan Dougherty, the manager." He eyed the wad of cash spilling out of her bag. Could it be counterfeit, he wondered? Better to play it on the safe side, he decided. "I'm afraid we don't have any openings at this time, but perhaps I could take your contact information and give you a call if anything becomes available."

"Oh no," Fiona moaned. "I was so hoping to stay here. I don't know if you've heard, but my brother accidently drowned in his pool last night."

"Yes. I'm so sorry, for your loss."

"The police have quarantined the house, so I can't go home." She covered her face with her hands and made some sobbing sounds.

Duncan looked to Patience, his eyes wide. *What should he do?*

Patience shrugged indiscreetly.

Fiona dropped slowly into a nearby chair. She held her head in her hands for a moment longer, then looked up abruptly. "Oh my," she said. "If I can't stay here, the camera crew will need to be notified." She opened the satchel and pulled out her cell phone.

"Camera crew?" Duncan asked.

"Yes, Channel 9 would like to interview me about my brother," she said, even though she hadn't actually scheduled that meeting yet. "I told them I'd be here, but I'll need to change that now." She clicked the button on the side of her phone.

The wheels in Duncan's head started turning. Free publicity for the hotel? This hotel being the choice of the great Artimus' sister? He reached out and held a hand over her phone. "No need to change the location for the interview, Miss Farkus. You're more than welcome to hold it here. We can get a conference room ready for you in a jiffy. What time is the interview?"

"Oh, that's very kind, but I just want to find a place to rest and clean up now. It's been a dreadful morning. And I don't want to be moving around from hotel to hotel." Fiona looked up at him. "I'm sure you understand."

He nodded slowly. "Yes, yes, of course. Hold still. Let me just double check and see what I can do." Duncan scurried off toward his office.

Not knowing what else to do, Patience followed. She closed the door behind them. "Do you think she's telling the truth?"

"I don't know, but if she is, and we pass up this opportunity, we'll be in big trouble." Duncan paced back and forth.

"She has lots of cash. We could get the money up front for the room in case she's lying."

"Good. But when you check her in, tell her we need to see her driver's license. Check the name and the address." He ran his fingers down his chin. "The great Artimus' last name was Farkus?"

Patience crinkled up her nose and shook her head. "That can't be right."

"Duncan shook his finger at her. "Look that up." He continued to pace. "Give her the suite on three."

"Good," Patience responded as she typed away on her cell phone. "She asked for a view of the lake."

"Get the fireside conference room ready, too – just in case."

"Here it is. Artimus Farkus," she read. "Huh. Who would know that?"

"The sister – or some quick-thinking scam artist," Duncan responded. "But you said she has cash. Just be sure to check the bills and let's do this!" He straightened his tie and stepped out the door.

CHAPTER 10

Meredith pulled her red Corvette into her garage stall and took a deep breath. She was exhausted. Getting rid of all the evidence was a huge task, but it was done now. No one ever need know the truth about the Artimus paintings. She just couldn't get over the irony of it all. If Art hadn't been blackmailing her, events certainly wouldn't have transpired as they did, and she wouldn't have gone down to his lair looking for the photos and found what she did – the repercussions of which would have changed their lives forever.

She tucked the car key fob into her purse and took a moment to scan the parking garage. Not a sole in site. Good. She made her way to the condo elevator and pushed the up arrow. But not a moment later, she heard a familiar voice behind her.

"Hello Meredith! How funny to run into you." The woman reached out and gave her an awkward hug. "I'm sure you're so distraught over Artimus' death. My, my what a tragedy!"

Ugh, Meredith thought to herself. The last thing she wanted was to have to talk with someone about the death of the great Artimus and hear them go on about how much they loved his work, blah, blah, blah, blah. And here was Irene Kipfer, the biggest busybody of them all. Irene had no husband, no children and little interest in anything except everybody else's business. "Irene! Where did you come from?" Meredith exclaimed, noticing that Irene looked like she had just woken up from a nap. One side of her face was a little rosy and the hair was sort of smashed to her head. Had she been waiting in her car for Meredith to arrive and fallen asleep?

"Oh, you know," Irene said. "Just getting home from some errands." She leaned in closer. "The condo is just humming with talk of Artimus' death." She shook her head. "They're all such busy bodies. I don't listen to all their gossip." She took Meredith by the arm. "But I'd like to hear the facts. What do you hear from the police?" She pushed the glasses up on her nose. "Was there foul play?"

"I'm afraid I've only heard as much as you, Irene." Meredith lowered her head to her chest. "It's just so sad. A great loss for the art world," she said in as sincere a voice as she could muster.

Irene lifted her painted-on eyebrows. "I hear he was having an affair with a married woman," she whispered loudly. She looked to Meredith for confirmation.

"Oh no, Irene. That's just all just media hype. Don't believe that for a second. Artimus was an upstanding man," she lied.

"He hit on me once," Irene said.

Meredith took a breath. She didn't doubt that. Art hit on every woman he met. "Well Irene, you're an attractive woman."

"But he never called."

"His life was indeed a busy one. Between creating his extraordinary works of art, world-wide showings and interview obligations, his plate was very full. I'm sure he would have once he had a minute." Meredith jabbed at the up arrow for the elevator again, hoping to make it come faster.

"It was three years ago."

"Ah well, time does fly, and as I said, he was a very busy man." She needed to change the subject, and quick. "So where did you say you were coming home from?"

"Oh, um…" She fluffed up her matted down hair. "Target," she said, then leaned close to Meredith's ear with a mischievous smile on her face. "I'll bet it was a jealous husband."

Meredith ignored the last comment. "Target? No luck?"

Irene blinked. "What?"

"Well, maybe it's just me," Meredith said with a laugh. "But when I come home from Target, I usually have at least three bags full of things I didn't even know I needed."

The elevator door opened and Meredith stepped inside with Irene at her heels. Meredith quickly pushed the button for her floor. "I don't know what it is about that store," Meredith continued. "But I can't leave without spending at least fifty bucks. Last time I was there I think I spent over a hundred and I was just going in for some eggs and milk." She eyed the floor numbers above the elevator doors. "I think I bought a sweater and a couple fluffy pillows that time." She could feel the elevator slowing. "Since I don't see any bags in your hands, you must have much better self-control, than I do."

"Oh. Right. Well, you know, they – they didn't have what I was looking for."

"I'm so sorry to hear that!" The door to the elevator opened and Meredith stepped out. "Better luck next time!" she called to Irene as the doors closed.

◆◆◆

Meredith entered the unit and placed her purse on the entryway table.

"Meredith?" came Dirk's voice from his office. "What took so long?"

She walked around the corner and leaned into the doorway. Dirk was standing in front of the wall-length window looking out over the Minneapolis skyline.

She went to him and hugged him from behind. "I had a lot of catching up to do," she said. "It was nice having the place to myself to get it all done."

He turned. "You look tired."

She nodded. "I am." Exhausted would have been a better word for how she was feeling. Trips up and down the stairway with box after box. Back and forth to the dumpster. She hadn't had a workout like that for a long time. No luck finding the photos, but she was certain that if the things she did find became public, it would put their gallery out of business. "Fortunately, the notice we posted kept the reporters away," she said. "But I was ambushed by Irene Kipfer at the elevator. I think she'd been sleeping in her car waiting for one of us to show up so she could get the latest scoop on the demise of the great Artimus. Can you believe it?"

"Exactly why I didn't leave the house today."

"Good choice."

"The phone has been ringing off the hook here. I stopped answering after I gave a statement to all the local news people."

"What a crazy thing, huh? So, what's the latest word?"

He shrugged. "It's all over the board. Lots of speculation about his death. Absurd stuff." He started pacing. "First, they'll compare him to Van Gogh, Degas and Munch and bring up research suggesting that the line between creativity and insanity is a fine one which is why so many of the great artists end up taking their own lives." Dirk paused and scowled. "I'll agree that Art was mentally deranged, but he'd never take his own life – at least on purpose." In fact, Dirk had pretty convincing evidence that Art would take someone else's life if it meant keeping his own. He started pacing again. "Then they'll talk about his playboy reputation, hinting that perhaps there was a vengeful, discarded girlfriend or murderous, jealous husband."

"That's where Irene is putting her money," Meredith interjected.

He paused again and raised his eyebrows. "Do you think there's a husband out there that should be jealous?"

"I'm sure they are numerous."

He nodded, then continued pacing. "And of course, there's always the nefarious conspiracy theories with envious artists who don't want to compete with him anymore, or art collectors who believe his art will increase in value after his death – you know, the usual web of intrigue and skullduggery. I tell you, the media is loving it."

"I'll bet. But whatever is discovered, I hope it doesn't lower the value of his paintings," Meredith said. And she had worked hard toward that end today.

"I honestly couldn't care less about that," Dirk responded gruffly.

♦♦♦

It was over ten years ago when Dirk first set eyes on Artimus Farkus. Actually, he heard him before he ultimately saw him.

"What the fuck is this? Why the hell do I have to take the bottom bunk?" Art shouted as he entered the barracks. "I can't squeeze in there! Shit! Who the hell took this top bunk?"

Dirk came out from the bathroom, toothbrush still in hand. He looked at Art. Just another blustering soldier, scared to be on the front lines, trying to keep it together by taking control of something. In this case, his bunk assignment. "I did," Dirk said.

Art lumbered toward him, then pointed his arm back toward the bunk. "I can't sleep on the bottom bunk," he shouted. "I'm a hefty guy. I gotta have space!"

Dirk shrugged. "Okay. Take the top."

'Yeah, that's right!" Art cheered. "I'm large and in charge!" He pitched his duffle across the room landing it on the top bunk. "Score! Woop! Woop! Woop! And the crowd goes wild!" He walked toward the bunk, arms held high over his head like a prizefighter.

Dirk honestly didn't care which bunk he had, so it was no skin off his back — at least at that moment. He walked over and extended his hand to Art. "I'm Dirk," he said.

Art slapped his hand away. "Okay, jerk – I mean Dirk, keep your shit to yourself and if you snore, I'm going to body slam you, got it?"

It seemed that Dirk's kind concession only ended up fanning Art's fire. And Art never missed an opportunity to belittle Dirk from that day forward. And each and every day, it made Dirk hate Art exponentially more. Art was a high-school bully who treated Dirk like a grade schooler. Only once did Dirk think he had bested Art, but Art turned the tables on him as usual.

It was the night Art walked over to the mess table letting out audible bursts of gas on his way.

Dirk plugged his nose with his fingers. "Damn man! You smell like a garbage dump. Can't you take care of that in the bathroom, Fartie? I mean, Artie?"

Another squad member chimed in. "Yeah. You smell like shit, Fartie."

The rest of the squad started to snicker. One pointed Art's way "Artie- Fartie!"

And the chant began. "Artie-Fartie! Artie-Fartie! Artie-Fartie!"

It was childish, but for some reason, that made it even funnier. And sometimes soldiers just need a release, so this was just the thing. The whole battalion chimed in.

Art stood there listening, tray in hand, with a scowl on his face.

Small as it may be, Dirk reveled in that moment believing he had finally succeeded in a little payback by making Art a laughingstock in front of the whole Battalion.

But to Dirk's dismay, Art shouted out. "Yep! That's me. Artie-Fartie!" He pointed at Dirk. "So you better watch out, Jerk. Cross me, and you're gonna get gassed!"

This caused an uproar of laughter and applause, and in the end, Dirk was the butt of the joke.

If the value of Art's paintings plummeted, Dirk would only be sorry that Art wasn't around to see it.

◆◆◆

Dirk took Meredith's hands in his and gazed lovingly at her. She was everything to him. She had stood by him through all. Through his absence while he was in Afghanistan; his many surgeries and hospital stays since his return; and his recurring nightmares and flashbacks. All of which had changed the course of their future. "I missed you last night," he said.

A pang of guilt overtook her. She bit her lip. Was this the time to tell him? To come clean? How would she even begin? How could she explain it all? No, she decided. With all that had happened today, it could wait for a better time. She gave his hands a squeeze "Yeah, sorry, the movie ran late," she told him.

"Right." He let her hands drop and turned back toward the window. "So, how had it been with you and Art lately? I guess I haven't asked you about it for a while."

In fact, she thought to herself, he never asked about it. She shoved her hands in her pockets. "The usual."

"We'll just have to get through this media frenzy," he said. "Then we can get on with our lives without that parasite."

"Yeah." She walked over and stood by his side. "What do you think happened?"

"Me? I think he was drunk and fell into the pool."

She nodded. "Sounds right to me. But there's any number of people Art has offended. If it turns out someone killed him, the police will have their hands full interviewing them all. It could take years."

Dirk crossed his arms over his chest. "Maybe some jealous husband gave him a little shove."

"Wouldn't surprise me."

He turned and took her in his arms. "I love you so much."

She smiled up at him. "And I love you so much more, my dearest love."

"Your *dearest* love? You mean there are *other* loves?"

She leaned back and playfully slapped him on his chest. "Don't be silly. You are my one and only."

He looked into her eyes. "If I were one of those men who found out my wife was having an affair, I'd be totally devastated. I don't know what I'd do." He kissed her softly. "Please don't ever leave me."

She took his face in her two hands and looked deep into his eyes. "You're everything to me. I'd never leave you." She leaned into him and held him close, knowing she needed to tell him soon. Very soon.

CHAPTER 11

Fiona found the telephone number for Channel 9 and dialed. After a few rings, a pleasant female voice answered. "Fox Nine," she said. "How may I direct your call?"

"I'd like to speak with Mimi Winslow," Fiona told her.

"Just a moment," the woman said and pressed the hold button.

The calming on-hold music began playing. Fiona sat straight in her chair and practiced her prepared introduction over and over again for what seemed like an eternity until someone finally came back on the line.

"Mimi Winslow's office, this is Sally. How may I direct your call?"

"I'd like to speak with Mimi Winslow."

"May I tell her who's calling?"

"This is Fiona Farkus, sister of Artimus. I'm calling about an interview."

"Just a moment," Sally said, and pressed the hold button.

Fiona rested her chin on her fist and sighed as the on-hold music began playing again.

"Mimi!" Sally called out. "It's someone who says she's the sister of Artimus!"

Mimi's head popped up from the papers on the desk in front of her. "Artimus had a sister?"

"That's what she says."

"Well don't just sit there, look it up," Mimi instructed as she got up from her desk and scurried over to Sally.

Sally's fingers flew across the keyboard. She typed in Artimus Farkus.

Mimi watched over her shoulder. "Farkus? Artimus' last name was Farkus?"

"That's the last name the caller gave me. Here it is. Artimus Farkus, Painter. Who would have guessed?"

"What about a sister — or any other family for that matter?"

Sally typed 'Fiona Farkus.' "Someone by that name has a facebook page. But I don't see anything about a relationship with Artimus."

Mimi picked up the thin file on Artimus from her desk. "Strange that nothing in here says anything about his family. But he must have one. Everyone has one." In fact, there was surprisingly little information about anything other than his Paintings and the award of the medal of honor. "Why is there so little here? Why don't we know more about this man?"

"I know the team has been working on it since his body was found this morning," Sally said.

"Good. Make sure they really dig in. We need to become experts in all that is Artimus – his last name, where he's from, how he became an artist, and particularly, if he has a sister. Then, if Artimus does have a sister, we need to confirm that this caller truly is the one who is Artimus' sister and not some imposter. And, if she is who she says she is, have them unearth all they can about the sister. Got it?"

Sally nodded. "Got it."

"Give me the phone." Mimi took the phone and held it to her ear. "This is Mimi Winslow. To whom am I speaking?"

Fiona sat up straight. "This is Fiona Farkus, Mimi. I'm the sister of Artimus. Since I believe you to be the best reporter in the Twin Cities, I wanted to call to see if you'd be interested in an interview. I want to be sure my brother's tragic death is handled with dignity." Fiona smiled proudly. She had delivered her introduction perfectly.

"Ms. Farkus, my sincere condolences on the loss of your brother. He was an international treasure. I'd be honored to speak with you and learn more about your early days in, I'm sorry, what was the name of the town you two grew up in?"

Who cares about *that*, Fiona thought to herself. "It was Faribault," she said.

"Oh yes." 'Faribault' Mimi wrote on her note pad. "Ms. Farkus, did you have any other family members that would like to join us for this interview?"

"No, Mimi, I am the last of our family."

"Oh my, again, my sincere condolences." The last Farkus? She checked her notes. "Were you able to be there when your brother was awarded that great honor?"

Mimi was testing her. Vetting her. Of course, Fiona thought to herself, she should have expected that. "No Mimi, I was not able to be there when my brother was awarded the medal of honor. I was living with my aunt at the time and she had limited funds. I lived with her after our father died."

Mimi scribbled down the information. Helpful. "And what did you say was your father's name?"

This was getting tiresome. "I didn't say, but his name was Frank if you must know. Frank Farkus. Artimus' mother's name was Lydia and after she died, our father Frank married my mother whose name was Ava. Is that enough history for you?"

Uh oh. It seemed Miss Farkus was getting a little testy. "I'm sure this is a hard time for you, Dear."

Did she call her Dear? Fiona hated that. It always seemed so condescending. She took a deep breath. She needed this interview. "Yes, it is, Mimi. Can we save further questions for our interview?"

"Of course, Dear. When are you available?"

"How does ten a.m. tomorrow work?"

That should give them ample time to check out her story, Mimi thought to herself. "Yes, ten a.m. will work just fine. I'm looking forward to meeting you. Please arrive at the television studio fifteen minutes early so they can get you set up with the microphones and lighting. Do you need the address?"

The TV studio? No way. Fiona had her own plans for this interview and was not going to change them. "No, Mimi that doesn't work for me. I have a room at the Bayview Inn in Wayzata, so you'll need to come here."

"But we have everything we need here at the studio, Dear. I'm sure we can make you comfortable."

Fiona snarled. She took another deep breath. "I'm trying to stay away from the public until this all calms down a bit. I'm sure you can understand that, Mimi," Fiona said. "As I said, you'll have to come here. Just please make sure you bring a camera crew."

Not many got away with telling Mimi Winslow what to do, but if Ms. Farkus was truly who she said she was, this would be a great scoop. "Okay," Mimi agreed. "I'll try to get a crew together and be there a bit before ten a.m. tomorrow."

Fiona raised her eyebrows. She'd *try* to get a crew together? What's that nonsense? This was an opportunity to interview the sister of the great Artimus! "Just to be clear, Mimi, if there's no camera crew, they'll be no interview. Do you understand?"

Mimi bristled. Her eyes narrowed. "Understood," she said, neglecting to add her own proviso that there would be no interview until Ms. Farkus was fully vetted.

"Good. Patience at the front desk will direct you to the conference room."

Conference room? "Ms. Farkus, will there be other news crews there as well? We're really not interested in competing with others for this interview."

What a prima donna! "Mimi, as long as you arrive on time, you'll have the scoop."

"It's a deal, Ms. Farkus. See you at ten a.m. sharp."

"Ten a.m. sharp." Fiona ended the call and fell back on the king-sized bed. It was beginning!

♦♦♦

Mimi handed the phone back to Sally. "Very strange," she said.

"Was it really the sister?"

"Unknown. Could be just some thrill seeker trying to get on TV, but if it really was the great Artimus' sister, we can't pass up the opportunity to interview her. She confirmed that we'd have the scoop before all other networks."

"Excellent."

"She's staying at the Bayview Inn in Wayzata. Call the hotel and see if they took her license number — but make sure to do it discretely. And find out if Artimus had a Will or Trust or something. We need to know if this sister will be the heir to his fortune."

"You got it."

◆◆◆

Fiona picked up the receiver on the phone next to the bed and dialed for the front desk.

"Yes, Ms. Farkus?" Patience answered while frantically gesturing to Duncan to join her. "How may I help you?"

Duncan was at Patience's side within seconds. She tilted the phone so they could both get an ear on the receiver.

"Channel 9 will be here for an interview tomorrow morning at ten a.m.," Fiona said.

Patience and Duncan silently gave each other a high five.

"Please set up the conference room for me."

"Of course," Patience responded. "Would you like us to provide coffee? Donuts, perhaps?"

Fiona hadn't thought about that, but said "Sure, that'd be good. I'll also need a rolling clothing rack."

Patience and Duncan shared a wide-eyed look.

"Will you be leaving us?" Patience asked trying to keep the alarm from her voice.

Fiona laughed to herself. First they tried to get rid of her, and now they're worried she's leaving. How funny was that? "No. No, I won't be leaving," she assured her. "It's for the interview. I'll need a clothing rack in the conference room. A good one. Not one with wobbly wheels or that's crooked - you know - one that looks shiny and new."

CHAPTER 12

Isaac sat on their back deck under the shade of the awning watching the birds cool themselves in the large birdbath at the corner of their garden. Even at this hour the temperature was in the high eighties. With the watering ban, the yards were all a bit brown, the garden soil was as hard as concrete, the flowers in the garden drooped, and the leaves of the cottonwoods had turned their backs to the sun giving them a silvery hue.

Claudia stuck her head out the sliding glass door. "Didn't you get enough of this heat this afternoon?"

"In just a few months we'll be missing this temperature."

"Well maybe you will, but I sure won't. Come on in, it's time to eat."

"Wonderful." He stood and stretched. "What's for dinner?" he asked as he made his way to the house.

Claudia smiled. "A special treat."

Isaac entered the home to find his oldest daughter, Avery, setting the table, Jacob feeding Walter the dog, Isabelle sitting on the kitchen counter helping Edna cook, and Claudia mixing the salad. His heart swelled with joy. What a beautiful sight to see! The whole family working together. At just that moment, he felt extremely blessed. "Smells delicious!" he said.

"It's walleye fish, Daddy!" Isabelle announced. "Just like the loons eat."

"The animal guys came and got the loon from the pond today," Jacob called from the back hall. "They shot it with a dart. It was cool!" He bent down and gave Walter a dish of water. "That's what I want to do when I grow up," he announced.

"You do, huh?" Isaac responded.

"Ugh!" Thirteen-year-old Avery moaned. "He just wants to shoot things with tranquilizer darts."

"So what's wrong with that?" Jacob countered. "Dad shoots people with real guns. That seems like a lot worse than shooting with tranquilizer darts."

Isaac's mouth dropped open. "I don't just randomly shoot people."

"The boys at school think you do," Avery groused.

"Sit everyone!" Edna, in her infinite wisdom called. "Supper's ready!" She always knew when it was time to squelch squabbling.

At that, Isabelle hopped off the counter and ran to the table. "I want to be a loon when I grow up," she declared.

"Is that right," Isaac responded.

"They can swim underwater for five minutes!" Isabelle told him.

"That's a long time."

She grinned. "Yeah."

♦♦♦

After dinner, Isaac watched from the door as tiny Edna backed her car out of the driveway. Drivers following her must wonder if there was anyone behind the wheel, he thought to himself. He cringed as she passed by a bicycle that was left lying there wondering if he might hear a crunch, but she successfully navigated around it and headed off down the road.

Isaac went to the kitchen where Claudia was finishing up the dishes. "Do you think we should arrange for Edna to have an Uber or Lyft ride to get from here and back?"

Claudia smiled. "Are you worried she can't see over the steering wheel?"

"You read my mind."

"Well, first, she'd never stand for it. And second, I've ridden in her car. She may be tiny, but she's a good driver. Do you think I'd let her run our children around town if I had any doubts?"

"Never." He smiled to himself. Once again, his beautiful wife eased his worries with her sensible calmness.

Claudia folded up the dish towel and hung it next to the sink. "On that subject, are you able to take Avery to her counseling appointment on Thursday? I have a meeting with a client that I just can't reschedule and Edna will be busy chauffeuring Jacob and Isabelle to their soccer practices."

"Sure. What time?

"3:00."

"That will work. I have an appointment to go over some evidence with Vick in the morning. But I'm sure we'll be wrapped up before noon."

"Vick? Vick's back from California?"

"Yep."

"Oh, my word. He won't be replacing Tom as your partner, will he?"

"No, it's just during the time that Tom's out on vacation."

"Oh good." She gave him a hug. "I'm sorry you'll have to work with Vick in the meantime. I know that means you'll be doing the work of both of you."

"Yeah," Isaac agreed. "Especially bad timing for this latest investigation. Petruco is all over this one."

She raised her eyebrows. "Are you talking about the death of Artimus?"

"You know who Artimus is?"

She laughed. "Of course I do. Everyone knows who Artimus is."

Everyone, it seemed, but Isaac. "They do?"

"Oh honey." She patted his cheek. "He painted the picture that's hanging above our living room loveseat."

"He did?"

"Well, it's a print," she explained. "We couldn't afford an original. Originals sell for tens of thousands of dollars."

"Huh."

Claudia crossed her arms over her chest. "But you know," she said with crinkled brow, "I always thought Artimus was a woman."

Isaac rolled his eyes at that. "No, no, honey. Not a woman. A *woman-izer*."

She frowned then took his hand and led him into the living room.

Isaac stood in front of the painting realizing he'd never really looked at it before. Claudia did their decorating, and he was always happy with the finished product, but he never really looked at each item separately. Shame on him, he scolded himself. Especially when he knew she agonized over each choice — oftentimes to his dismay. Why don't you just pick something? he'd say to her. Who cares? It's not going to make a difference. But he was just now coming to the conclusion that he was mistaken. This was a very nice painting. It wasn't so much that it was of any particular "thing;" because it wasn't. It was more because of the emotions it evoked when looking at it. It was swirly. It made you feel warm, natural, peaceful. Such a strong contrast to the man named Artimus he was conjuring in his mind as the evidence came in.

Claudia sighed. "A womanizer you say? Really?"

He considered the evidence. Wet bikinis, pornography everywhere. "It would seem so," he said.

She furrowed her brow. "Wasn't Artimus a Greek Goddess?"

Isaac chuckled. "I don't know. I think I flunked Mythology."

"It just made sense to me that someone with the same name as a Greek Goddess would paint pictures like this. I guess I had it all wrong."

After seeing this painting, Isaac was wondering if he had it all wrong too.

CHAPTER 13

Darcy rolled over and checked her cell phone. Four a.m. She'd been tossing and turning since three o'clock thinking about what lay ahead in the wake of all that had happened. Unable to sleep, she got out of bed and began to prepare for the money drop. This would be the second time, and Darcy knew it was uncertain if it would be the last. Meredith was so naïve. Darcy shook her head. Such changes of fortune from one chance encounter. And even after all of this, it seemed that Meredith had no intention of stopping her extra-marital affair.

Darcy would never forget the day she delivered the first blackmail letter to Meredith only a month ago.

♦ ♦ ♦

Meredith had entered the office like she was riding on a cloud and floated over to Darcy's desk. "Hello, Darcy! How are you on this beautiful morning?"

"My, my, someone is happy today," Darcy responded.

"Is it that obvious?" Meredith gushed.

Darcy sat back in her chair. "What's gotten into you?"

Meredith giggled. "Just woke up on the right side of the bed today, I guess."

"Well good for you," Darcy said. She picked up the letters on her desk and handed them over. "Here's most of the mail, but there was an unusual letter addressed to you, individually, so I put it on your desk."

"Unusual letter? Whatever do you mean?"

Darcy sighed. "It's…" she began to try to explain, then stood up and took Meredith's arm. "Come on, I'll show you. It's just *different*."

Darcy watched as Meredith picked up the envelope.

"Hmmm. This is unusual." She let out a snort. "Looks like they used my grandmother's old typewriter." She flipped it over. "And there's no indication where this is from." She bounced it up and down in her hand. "It's thick too. Maybe some new artist is sending samples? Well, let's see."

Darcy watched as Meredith opened the letter and the photos fell out onto her desk.

Meredith gasped. "What in the world is this?" She started to read, and all the color drained from her face. She picked up the photos and stared at the images.

"You don't look so good," Darcy said. "Let me go get you some water."

Darcy returned a few minutes later.

Meredith sat at the desk with the letter and photos spread out before her.

Darcy set the glass down on the desk in front of her.

Meredith looked up at her. "I suppose you're wondering what this is all about," she said.

Darcy nodded sheepishly. "Yeah, but it's not my business."

"Well, you've already seen everything, so I think it *is* kind of your business now." Meredith rubbed her temples. "Besides, I have a big favor to ask you."

"Oh, don't worry, Meredith. I swear I won't tell anyone about this. I promise," Darcy said. Then she cringed. "Are you being blackmailed?"

Meredith got up from her desk and walked across the room to the window. "Yeah, I guess I am."

"Geez. For what?" Darcy dropped into the chair on the other side of Meredith's desk. "I mean if you don't mind me asking."

"There's a man I've been seeing." Meredith turned and pointed at Darcy. "It's not what you think."

"Okay. But, I mean, if it's not what I think, then why would someone be blackmailing you for it?"

The question hung in the air for several minutes. Meredith looked to the sky. "I can't explain that."

Sure she could, Darcy thought to herself, but she probably just didn't want to. "Okay. So…. do you love him?" she asked.

"Oh no, it's not like that." Meredith reached up and closed the blinds.

"Then why?"

"Because he's…." Meredith paused, searching for the right word. "Perfect," she finally said.

Darcy squawked. "Right. So how did you happen to meet Mr. Perfect?"

Meredith leaned her back against the wall. "I saw him at the mall."

"You met at the mall?"

"Yes." Meredith's eyes lit up. "It was just fate. I turned away from the cosmetics counter and he ran right into me." Meredith sighed. "I tell you, I just couldn't believe my eyes. He was perfect."

There was that word again. "Perfect? You keep saying that, but you didn't even know him! How could he be *perfect*?"

"His height, his build, his blonde, wavy hair — and those brown eyes." She shook her head as if in disbelief. "He was perfect."

"So, do you think he ran into you on purpose? Did he come on to you?"

"Oh no." She shook her head. "He very politely said "So sorry, miss, please excuse me," and went on his way."

"But I couldn't take my eyes off of him. I – I – I just followed him."

"You were stalking him?"

"Not stalking, *following.*"

"Did he notice you were *following* him?"

"No, I don't think so."

"You realize this is a little creepy, right?"

"I know. But I couldn't help myself. I needed him. I wasn't going to let him get away."

"You needed him?"

"Yes, I needed him," Meredith said with conviction. "Anyway, when he got in line at the food court, I got in line behind him."

"You're kidding me. Did he notice you then?"

"He did when I tapped him on the shoulder."

"Did he remember you?"

"Oh yes. He apologized again for running into me and asked if I was hurt. Can you believe that? He was so kind. Such a gentleman. He was perfect." Her hands went to her heart. "I think he was wondering why I was tapping him on the shoulder. So, I told him that I had a proposal for him and asked if he would like to join me for dinner."

"So, *you* pursued *him?*"

"Yes. And he was nice enough to take the time for me."

"He was *nice* enough?"

"He was an answer to my prayers. A gift from God. Like he was just dropped out of the sky for me." Meredith walked back across the room and took her seat. "So here's the big favor I need from you." She looked into Darcy's eyes. "I'd like you to help me deliver the money."

Darcy raised her brows. "What?"

"Well, not *deliver* the money exactly. I'd like you to watch the drop off spot, to see who *picks up* the money."

Darcy nodded. "Okay."

♦♦♦

That's how it began. And Darcy did as she was asked. She stayed at that drop off spot all morning. When Meredith called to check in three hours later, Darcy told her she hadn't seen anyone come and collect the money. So, Meredith went back to look and found that the money was gone.

It was a mystery, Darcy said. She swore to Meredith that she was there the entire time, but she also explained that there had been a lot of traffic and had to admit that someone could have slipped in unobserved. She was pretty sure Meredith had believed her, but most decidedly, Darcy was more than happy *not* to be the one on the lookout today.

CHAPTER 14

Avery woke again with night terrors. They had been getting less and less over time, but the events of last spring still haunted her. Isaac didn't know if it was the sight of the badly decomposed dead body she'd landed on, or the groping hands of the boy who had taken her there in the woods that fateful day that frightened her more, but both still haunted Isaac as well. Without a doubt, seeing his own daughter step out of the back seat of the squad car after having discovered a dead body had been the hardest event of his life. They said her scream could be heard for miles.

He'd soothed her back to sleep, but knew sleep wasn't in the cards for him at this hour. He slipped out the sliding glass door, set his coffee on the table, opened his laptop and stretched his arms to the sky.

All in all, he did enjoy spending the early morning on the deck in these summer months when the sun begins to peek over the horizon at 5 a. m. and the pink, orange and yellow light begins to fill the sky. Claudia would be up soon going about her usual routine getting ready for work, but the kids would sleep in enjoying their summer vacation. Theirs was a busy household and Isaac reveled in these quiet moments.

The barn swallows who built their mud nest under the decking flew up and called out to alert others in the area to the intruder above. Isaac watched as they gathered from all over the neighborhood. It was impossible to count them as they flitted about, deftly rolling through quick turns and diving in close to scare him away. Their comradery and teamwork was very impressive, albeit annoying. But from past experience he knew they'd settle down after a while if he just kept reasonably still.

He hit the power button on his laptop and watched as it came to life, hoping Cynthia's autopsy report came in today and praying that she had been able to determine that Artimus' death had been a tragic accident. Then the entire world could come together and honor, praise and give tribute to this world renown artist, and lay him to rest with dignity.

If not, and from all the gossip that had already begun to be reported as "news," Isaac knew they were in for it. It would be the most highly publicized, scrutinized, criticized case he had ever had. He was sure every step they took would be disapproved of, second-guessed, and/or misinterpreted by somebody-or-other sensationalizing the murder of this Van Gogh of the 21st century.

He opened his Outlook program, and there it was. A message from Cynthia Chu. He cringed as he clicked on it, then let out a big sigh. Sadly, she had not yet submitted her report. All the message said was, "I need to talk to you." His head dropped into his hands.

"You okay, daddy?" came a voice from inside the screen door.

He looked up to see his youngest, Isabelle. "I'm fine, honey. What are you doing up so early?"

She shrugged, opened the door, and padded over to him in her bare feet. She hopped up onto his lap, gave him a big hug, then held his cheeks in her two tiny hands. "Why are you sad, daddy?"

He chuckled. She could read him like a book. "Well honey, somebody died, so I'm sad about that."

"Was it the arty miss?"

He blinked. "Well yes it was. How did you know about Artimus?"

She dropped her hands into her lap. "Mommy and Edna were talking about her. She paints pictures," she told him. "I guess that's why they call her the arty miss." She looked up at him with wide eyes. "They said she was in a pool."

Isaac nodded.

"Did she get shot with a tranquilizer gun?"

"No, honey. Tranquilizer guns are only for animals."

Her eyes grew even wider. "Did you shoot her daddy?"

"No honey, nobody got shot."

The door opened and Claudia stepped onto the deck. "Miss Isabelle," she said. "What are you doing out here?"

"Daddy's sad about the arty miss."

Claudia furrowed her brow. "What?"

"Artimus," Isaac said with a smile. "The death of Artimus"

Claudia laughed. "Ah."

◆◆◆

It was seven o'clock by the time Isaac arrived at the station. News vehicles filled the parking lot. As he stepped out of his car, reporters ran toward him shouting questions.

"Detective Scott, was Artimus murdered?"

"Did he commit suicide?"

"When will the Examiner's report be in?"

"Have you seen it?"

Isaac held his hands up and hurried toward the door. "No comment." He'd happily let Petruco handle all of this.

He set up in the meeting room, picked up the phone, and dialed Cynthia.

"Good morning, Isaac," Cynthia said.

"Good morning, Cynthia. I received your message."

"Yes. I wanted you to be the first to know. I have good evidence to conclude this drowning was not accidental."

"I appreciate the heads up. May I ask what you've found that suggests this?"

"It will all be in my report. I'm just waiting on the toxicology results to finish it up, but they work at the speed of sloths down there."

"I look forward to receiving the report, Cynthia, but if you would allow me just a few minutes of your valuable time to enlighten me on what kind of evidence you've found, it would be very helpful with my investigation."

"My time *is* valuable, Isaac," Cynthia responded. "That you understand that, is the reason I am willing to grant your request. But you must not hold me to any of this until the toxicology results are in and confirmed."

"Understood."

"As you know, my examinations are thorough and unparalleled. I am only giving you this information prior to the release of my final report because I don't want any time wasted. You must investigate this as a homicide.

However, you must not reveal any of what I am about to tell you. Agreed?"

"Agreed."

"Fine. Here are the main concerns, and I'll try to put them in lay person's language so that you can understand. First, his pupils were dilated indicating he was under the influence of some kind of drug. Second, the cloudiness of his corneas indicates his eyes were open when he drown. But most importantly, the presumptive tests show the victim had been drinking alcohol and had very high levels of TCAs."

"TCAs?"

"Tricyclic antidepressants. Granted, Artimus could have been taking this on a regular basis to help with depression, and we will be able to know if the use was chronic once his hair analysis is in, but in my review of the report of the search on the victim's residence, no prescription bottles – empty or otherwise – were found. Where did he get it? Why did he have so much in his system?"

"How much? Enough to kill him? Could it be suicide?"

"Not enough to kill him, but enough to make him very confused and drowsy - practically immobile."

"If he was immobile, how did he get in the pool?"

"Exactly," Cynthia said. "He also had a contusion on the left side of his face. I can't be certain that this didn't happen in a fall, or by those idiot divers who pulled the body out of the pool, but because the blood vessels are fairly diffuse and widespread around the area of impact, it looks like he was struck prior to the time he entered the pool."

"Struck? With a tool? A fist?"

"Let's say, a fist-sized object. So Isaac, until you find out where Artimus got the antidepressant, I can't determine if this was suicide or homicide, but it is certain, it was not accidental."

Isaac ran his hand over his face. A homicidal overdose almost always involved someone close to the victim. Someone who knew his habits. Someone he would trust to hand him a beverage or some food. "I appreciate the information, Cynthia." Did he? In reality, he would have preferred to hear a much different report – one that didn't suggest foul play.

"You're welcome. I expect you to proceed, keeping what we discussed confidential."

"Of course."

"When will Detective Bryant be back? You're going to need him on this one."

Isaac shook his head. Poor Tom. He had to pity anyone that took Cynthia's fancy. It was like trying to dodge a bullet. "I believe he will be back the beginning of next week."

"Well, when he returns, please let him know I'll be ready to meet with him to get him up to speed on the case."

"How kind of you. I will let him know."

♦♦♦

Thanks to Cynthia, they now had a lead. The pills were the key. So, if they weren't at his house or in his car, there had to be another place to search. He googled the name "Artimus" on his computer. Pictures of his paintings popped up with the address to the gallery showcasing them right here in Minneapolis. He picked up the phone. "Peg, can you find out who owns the gallery at 220 First Street? I need the phone number. And when Vick gets in, please send him to me."

"I'll find out the owner," she said with a giggle. The kind of giggle only Vick could evoke in women. "And Vick's right here. I'll send him down."

A few minutes later, the door to the meeting room swung open with a bang.

"Vick. How nice of you to show up to work today."

Vick smoothed the hair back over his head. "Hey, I was trying to get through the hordes of reporters out there. I thought I was going to get tackled by some of them. You'd think we were holding Taylor Swift in here."

"Yeah, well let's get this investigation going." Isaac tapped his pencil on the table. "Have a seat."

Vick twirled the chair around and straddled it. "At your service, Magnificent One."

"When I spoke with Fiona yesterday, she said that usually there were dishes left for her to clean, but there weren't any this last time. We need to know more about that – and anything else that was out of the ordinary." He pulled out his notebook and started to make a list. "Did she notice anything missing in the home? What can she tell us about Artimus' health? Was he taking any anti-depressants? What was his state of mind? Who were his friends? Did he have any enemies? Why was there money hidden all over the house? Did she know about that? Does she know if he had any bank accounts?" He ripped off the page and handed it to Vick. "You know the drill. Find out anything and everything you can about Artimus – and their relationship as well. She said they were close, but she stands to inherit his fortune."

Vick grinned. "Oh yeah, and what a fortune."

"Since she seems to trust you, see if you can meet up with her today." Isaac jotted her cell phone number on the top of the page. "I'm going to the gallery and see what we can find out there." He stood to go get the gallery information from Peg and pointed to the phone number. "Give her a call," Isaac instructed.

Vick pulled the cell phone from his pocket and dutifully dialed.

♦ ♦ ♦

Isaac returned momentarily with the gallery information in hand. "So?" he asked.

"She said she didn't have time to talk with me this morning," Vick said. "We'll be having lunch at her hotel instead."

Isaac's eyes narrowed. "Vick," he said. "No dating her. We're in the middle of an investigation."

Vick held up his hands like he was under arrest. "Hey, she set this up – not me."

Isaac stared at Vick a little longer. "She's like 20 years old, you know."

"So? I can't help it if she's in to me. I have a magnetism that transcends age."

Isaac pointed a finger at him. "No dating her while this investigation is active."

"Well of course. Not *now*. But once this is over, I wouldn't mind hanging out with the heir to the great Artimus' fortune and help her spend a little of that money."

"Seriously? I thought you were all about your image, and you're telling me you would be seen out in public with a child in a sparkly slasher dress?"

Vick smiled and shook his head. "I don't care about all those glittery clothes, Isaac. I'm a naturalist. I only care about the body underneath."

CHAPTER 15

Meredith pulled her Corvette into the stall next to Darcy's car. How she wished Darcy had never learned of this, but on the other hand, Darcy had been a great help to her. Hopefully this time it would work out as she expected, and she would be able to collect her money and stop worrying about the blackmailer – who she was still convinced was Art. The problem was, she didn't have proof of it. For some reason she expected Art to have prints of the photos at the ready to humiliate Dirk on a moment's notice. But she hadn't been able to locate the damning photos in his lair. Perhaps he kept them at his home or in a safe deposit box somewhere? Hopefully whoever found them would think nothing of them – just a picture of a couple having dinner, nothing more. After all, with Art out of the picture, the only one who would know differently would be Dirk. And so as long as the pictures weren't at the gallery, Dirk wouldn't have access to them and would never have reason to see them. She puffed out her cheeks and let out a long sigh because she knew, down deep in her heart, that what she really needed to do was confess.

She saw Darcy rounding the back of her Corvette. "Hey girl!" Meredith said as she got out of her car. "Thanks so much for doing this for me."

"Sure," Darcy responded.

Meredith reached out and gave Darcy a hug.

"Did you bring the raincoat?" Darcy asked.

Meredith opened the trunk and pulled it out. "Right here. And here's the floppy hat and a pair of my shoes."

Darcy grimaced. "I'm going to look ridiculous."

Meredith smiled. "You'll look like me."

"There's not a drop of rain expected today." She pointed toward the entrance. "Did you see the sun shining outside?"

Meredith slapped her forehead with the heal of her hand. "Oh, right! Thanks for the reminder." She took the sunglasses off the top of her head. "Wear these too."

"A raincoat and sunglasses. That makes sense."

"They'll help hide our different facial features."

"Sure," Darcy responded sounding unconvinced.

A buzzing noise came from Darcy's pocket.

"What's that?" Meredith asked.

Darcy reached in and silenced the alarm. "I'm keeping us on time. The way I figure it, you should leave in 5 minutes so you can have a chance to get a good viewing spot."

"Good thinking!"

Darcy put on the coat and hat. "Don't let your guard down," she said to Meredith. "It's a busy time of day, lots of people busing to work and more traffic on the roads making it easier for someone to get away with the money."

"Not on my watch. I won't let that money out of my sight," Meredith said as she handed Darcy the bag of cash.

♦♦♦

Meredith looked at her cell phone again. Two hours had passed, and she hadn't seen anyone at the trash can. This was enough. The only one it could have been was Art, she assured herself for the millionth time, and he was gone now. It was time to go collect her money.

But just as she opened the car door, her phone rang. She pulled the door closed and answered. "Hi my love."

"Hi Meredith," Dirk replied. "I got a call from a police detective. He said he stopped by the gallery this morning, but the door was locked and no one answered when he rang the bell. Aren't you there?"

"Oh no, didn't I tell you?" She searched her mind for a good excuse. "I–I had a doctor appointment this morning," she lied.

"A doctor appointment? Oh Meredith, I wish you would've let me know about that. I'd like to go with you. We're in this together, remember?"

"You're so sweet." She rubbed her forehead. "With all that was going on yesterday with Art's death, it must have slipped my mind. I promise to let you know next time." If there was a next time, she thought to herself.

She sounded stressed, he thought sadly. The last thing he wanted to do was cause her more stress. "Okay. Good." He frowned. "Did it go okay?

"Yes, yes. Everything is fine."

As much as he wanted this, he wouldn't push her. "You know, you don't have to go forward with this if you don't want to."

"Don't be silly, sweetheart. Of course I want to. I'm not saying that." She let the side of her head fall against the car window. "I just think we should wait and see what happens this time." She needed to change the subject. "I'll be back at the gallery shortly," she told him. "I'm assuming this police business has to do with Art, right?"

"Yes. That's right. The officer wants to see Art's space. I gave him permission to look at whatever he wants," Dirk told her. "I mean I can't imagine that there'll be much to see – other than empty beer cans and pornography."

If he only knew, she thought to herself. And even though she had already done this, she said, "I'll go down there and tidy it up a bit."

"No. Don't do that. The more I think of it, the more I think Art should be remembered for exactly the kind of person he was. I don't know why we keep sugar coating his reputation, do you?"

"Well, honey," she said softly, knowing the subject of Artie Farkus always stirred him up. "It will help keep the value of his art at a high level."

"That's it?"

"Yes. I mean, we've invested a lot in it. I'd like to protect his memory."

There was silence on the other end.

"Okay," she whispered. "Please text me the officer's number. I'll give him a call and set up a time to meet."

"Good. What time are you coming home?"

"I guess it will depend on how long it takes with the police, but I'll keep you updated."

"Good."

They disconnected and Meredith let out a long sigh. Poor Dirk. She knew how hard it was for him to heap praises on the person he hated most in the world. She would just have to cover for him.

She hopped out of the car and moved swiftly through the heat waves radiating off the pavement, across the parking lot, to the bus stop. She ran around to the trash can at the back. She peered inside. The money was gone.

CHAPTER 16

It had been an interesting conversation with the gallery owner, Mr. Stanton, Isaac thought to himself. He had been more than surprised to learn that no one was here at the gallery, and when Isaac requested permission to search the premises, he seemed almost eager for it. What had he said? "Yes, search away. I'm sure you'll find all kinds of dreadful and nasty things." Dreadful things? *Nasty* things? In all his years, Isaac had never heard someone relishing the thought of such findings. Needless to say, Isaac was now quite eager to get started — and the best news was that there would be no need for a search warrant. The police would have free access to all.

He opened the car door, pulled off his blazer, and draped it over the back seat. The stand alone, two-story red brick building with its gently arched windows looked to be built in the 1880s before the skyscrapers to the south filled the downtown area. The large sign with italicized lettering across the front identified it as "*Perceptions.*" It fronted on First Street with Second Avenue on the side. An alleyway separated it from the building next door. The windows on the alley side of the building were covered by dark shades and all the window wells were blacked out. In contrast, the gallery on the Second Avenue side was brightly lit and filled with colorful paintings, and sculptures made of a variety of materials from iron, clay, brass, used motor parts and the like. All new and modern. No Whistler's Mother or Mona Lisa here. He was surprised that he was able to identify the paintings by Artimus. He did indeed have a certain style. A natural style. Where did he paint these, Isaac wondered. There wasn't a studio, or any art materials in Artimus' home.

Isaac took a look at his watch. According to Ms. Stanton, she would be there soon to open the gallery, so he decided to take advantage of this little bit of privacy and investigate the perimeter. Isaac truly appreciated the opportunity to start the search on his own without interference. He found it beneficial to view the site, undisturbed, before the rest of the team arrived. This allowed him to get the best insights about a case, and the quiet atmosphere helped him follow those instincts – and Isaac Scott had a well-known and highly respected track record for having great instincts. He also had a lot of experience under his belt, and while he would be the first to say that experience helped, he knew all too well it couldn't replace the nagging, subconscious, intuition cops referred to as "hunches."

He got back in his car, pulled around to the alleyway behind the gallery, and parked in the shade created by the building. With this intense heat, it probably wouldn't help much, but anything was better than parking in the sun. Bits of garbage littered the alley. The dumpster sat to his left. Isaac knew that a dumpster could hold all kinds of evidence and his greatest hope at this moment was that it held an empty bottle of TCAs prescribed to Artimus Farkus.

He pulled down his sleeve to protect his hand, lifted the steaming hot metal cover, and let it fall to the side. He peered over the edge. The dumpster was almost full. A stack of pornographic magazines sat on top of an old overhead projector on the far side. Numerous boxes of floor tiles were strewn about, along with several garbage bags of beer cans and alcohol containers and the usual office waste. He thought he could make out an old printer near the bottom of the pile, and thin strips of plastic that were spilling out of a Target bag. He wiped the perspiration from his forehead. The forensics team would have their work cut out for them, diving in and sorting through. Unfortunately, he didn't see any prescription bottles, but they could easily be hidden in the midst of all that trash, or even better, be found inside the gallery.

He got back in his car, turned the air-conditioning on high and dialed the precinct. "Peg, I'm here at the gallery," Isaac said as he mopped the sweat from the back of his neck with a tissue. "We have the go ahead to search the site from the owner. Would you please get a forensics team together?"

"Will do, Isaac."

"Please tell them to do their best to slip out without alerting the press."

"Shouldn't be too much trouble," she chuckled. "Petruco is out there addressing them right now and, as always, he has their full attention."

"Great. Ask the team to start on the outside perimeter and the dumpster in the back."

"Outside? Oh, they'll love that," she said sarcastically. "Must be a hundred degrees out there."

"Believe me, I am aware."

◆ ◆ ◆

Meredith ran back to the car and called Darcy in a panic. "Aren't you at the gallery?" she asked.

"No," Darcy replied. "I'm at the Caribou down the road. I thought you might like me to bring you your car after you collect the money. Did you get it?"

Meredith sighed. "No."

"How much longer are you going to wait?"

Meredith let out a frustrated scream. "I didn't get it, because it's gone."

"Gone?"

"Yes."

"Did you see who picked it up?"

"No. I didn't see anyone. I don't know how they could have slipped by me."

"I'm so sorry, Meredith," Darcy said. Undoubtedly Meredith now knew that the blackmailer was someone other than Art, she thought to herself. "Should I come there?" Darcy asked.

"Yes, please. We need to get back to the gallery. The police want to search it."

"The police? Can they do that? Don't they need a search warrant?"

"No, Dirk gave them permission."

CHAPTER 17

Fiona stood in front of the full-length mirror and admired herself. This was the look the women of the Twin Cities, and soon the whole world, would be clambering for. "Thank you, Art," she said aloud. "Finally, a little pay-back." After all, he wouldn't have been anything if it hadn't been for her. But now it was her time.

Stepping out of the elevator in the lobby, she found the camera crew setting up in front of Art's painting. "No, no, no," she said to the cameraman, her arms crossing back and forth in front of her like a football referee. "Not here. You're supposed to be in the conference room over there."

"Hey, I'm just doing what Mimi told me to do," the cameraman answered. "You'll have to take it up with her."

Patience stepped up beside her. "I told them they were to be in the conference room, but they didn't listen," she said.

"Where's Mimi?"

"She went to the powder room." Patience said gesturing down the hallway. "Oh wait, here she comes!"

"Mimi!" Fiona shouted. "Your crew is in the wrong place."

Mimi held out her hand. "You must be Fiona."

Fiona took her hand. "Yes, but your crew is setting up in the wrong place. We have the conference room ready."

"It is an honor to meet the sister of the great, too-soon-to-be-departed Artimus." Mimi gave her a sad smile.

Fiona wanted to gag. "Yeah, thanks. But Mimi, you've got to move your crew."

Mimi held her hands high as though they were holding the painting behind her. "What a perfect backdrop," Mimi exclaimed. "One of Artimus' originals! I knew you wanted us to come here for the interview for a reason."

"No," Fiona growled. "No, that isn't right." Mimi was smooth, but Fiona was not to be moved. "We need to have you set up in the conference room."

Mimi looked over at the cameraman. "You set Josh?"

"All set, Mimi," he replied.

"Well, see there?" Mimi said to Fiona. "We're already all set. Why don't we just move on from here."

Fiona narrowed her eyes. "Move to the conference room, Mimi, or no interview." She crossed her arms over her chest. "I'm sure Channel 11 can be here in minutes," she added.

Mimi pursed her lips. She didn't care for being told how to run an interview, but she knew *this* interview was going to be mind-blowing, no matter where it was held. "As you wish," she said to Fiona, then snapped her fingers at Josh and pointed down the hall. "Let's move it, boys."

Fiona led the way and the crew followed.

Fiona had the room set up so that the rolling rack of clothes would have the backdrop of a windowless wall to avoid any sun issues, and two chairs were placed directly in front for the interview. "I'll sit here and you can sit there," she told Mimi.

Mimi snapped her fingers again to direct the crew. She walked around the rolling rack. "What's all this?"

"My wearable art creations," Fiona responded. "Art – Artimus, as you know him, was investing in my project."

"*Really.*"

"Yes, he was my biggest supporter," she lied. "He loved them so much he funded my whole project. I know he'd want me to share these with you in the interview." She picked up a piece of paper from the chair. "I'd like you to ask these questions about them."

Mimi took the page and looked at the questions. "Forgive me," she said. "But I'm a bit confused."

"Oh?"

"Yes. Is this interview about you or your brother, the great Artimus?"

Fiona gave her a smile. "It's about the great Artimus' legacy – which happens to be me."

♦♦♦

Mimi smiled at the camera. "Today we are here at the Bayview Inn for an exclusive interview with Fiona Farkus, the sister of international treasure, Artimus, who tragically passed away just yesterday," she told the viewers. She turned toward Fiona. "Our condolences, Fiona. I'm sure this is a difficult time for you."

Fiona nodded. "Thank you, Mimi."

"We all know of his great artistry, but I'd like to dig a bit deeper into your family history." The truth was, she could hardly wait to get to it. But first she knew she would have to get Fiona comfortable. "What insights can you give the viewers about your brother as a person?"

Fiona couldn't have asked for a better introduction. She smiled at the camera. "Well, my brother was very excited about my line of wearable art." She gestured at the clothing hanging on the rack behind her. "In fact, before his unexpected death, I think it was the thing he was most passionate about."

Unbelievable, Mimi thought to herself. But no matter. She was willing to indulge this childish self-promotion for a bit before getting to the meat of the interview, because she knew the meat was going to be really tasty and worth waiting for. Her team had outdone themselves. "Is that right?" Mimi said.

"Yes. Art always said that I was the true artist in the family."

"Well, then." She smiled. "Please, show us some of your creations."

Fiona stood. "These are all hand-crafted, one-of-a-kind pieces." She did a little twirl to show off the dress she was wearing. "As you can see the embellishments are on both the front and the back. The gemstones and glitter are imported from Italy." She held up an example and turned the hangar back and forth in her hand scattering glitter. "This was one of Art's favorites," she lied.

"I see," Mimi said as she brushed some of the glitter off her skirt. She looked down at the list of questions Fiona had given her. "How would one go about ordering the pieces?" she read in staccato.

"Well Art thought we should open a gallery of sorts where people could come, see, and touch my clothing de-signs. I say gallery, because my clothing designs are not available off the rack like in clothing stores, but are indi-vidual pieces of art that can be ordered to meet the clients specific design choices."

"So, the two of you planned to open a gallery?"

"Yes, that's right," she said to Mimi, then looked toward the camera. "And I intend to go forward with it on my own because I know it would be Art's wish that I do so."

"It sounds like you two were very close."

"Yes. We were. And I plan to show and sell his paintings in my shop as well," she added. That ought to get some butts in the door, she thought to herself.

"A lot of excitement for you in the wake of your brother's death."

"Yes," Fiona said with a smile, then quickly replaced it with a frown. "But of course, I'd rather he be here to see it."

"Of course." Mimi sat straighter in her seat. Now to get to the meat, she thought eagerly. "As you told me earlier, you are the sole heir to Artimus' legacy. May I ask you some questions about your family history?"

"Sure."

"So, you are the last of the Farkus family."

"Sadly, yes. That's true."

"And you and Artimus share a father, is that correct?"

"Yes, that's right. Art's mom departed when he was young. Afterward, Art's dad married my mom." She put on a somber face. "They're both dead now too."

"Very sad. First Artimus' mother, then your mother, then the death of your father — and now your brother is gone. Tragic."

Fiona bowed her head and nodded.

"But you're leaving out some important details."

"I am?"

"Your father was Frank Farkus, is that right?"

"Yes. That's right."

"Frank Farkus who was married to Lydia who was Artimus' mother?"

"Yes, that was her name. It was quite a bit before my time, though." She rubbed her forehead. *Why was she wasting time on this?*

"Lydia who disappeared when Artimus was only eight years old and whose body was found in the woods not far from where your father liked to go hunting?"

Fiona could feel the tension rising in her throat. "Really? I didn't know that." *Why was she going there?*

"Her body was so badly decomposed they couldn't confirm the cause of death."

Fiona shifted in her seat. *What was happening?*

"In fact, so badly decomposed," Mimi continued, "that the police couldn't find enough evidence to charge your father with her murder, but the records show they were certain that was the case."

Creases appeared on Fiona forehead. "What? Are you sure, Mimi? That doesn't sound right."

"Then two years later your father married Ava, who was your mother, is that right?"

"Yes."

"And you were born a few years after that."

"Uh huh."

"When you were eight your mother died suddenly."

"Yes, bless her soul."

"And in fact, your father was charged with her murder."

Fiona gulped. She felt like she couldn't breathe. "No," she cried. "No, that's not true."

"Oh yes, it's true."

"I – I've never heard anything like this." Fiona said, wringing her hands.

"Your mother died of ingesting a lethal amount of rat poisoning."

"She did? Wh-Where did you hear this?" The tears started to roll down her face. "I didn't know any of this." She looked at the camera, eyes wide. "I was eight!"

"And your father lost the farm after spending all his money defending himself in her murder trial."

Fiona let her head drop into her hands.

"Then he hung himself."

"Yes," she whispered.

"Now the autopsy results show that Artimus was also poisoned."

Fiona's head popped up, mascara running down her cheeks. "What?" She clenched her fists. "Where are you getting your information?"

Mimi looked straight into the camera lens. "We have a copy of the presumptive test showing Artimus had large amounts of antidepressants in his system." She held up a document to the camera. "What an interesting coincidence. Another poisoning leading to death in the Farkus family." She turned her gaze to Fiona. "The question is, sole heir to Artimus' fortune, did you follow in your father's footsteps?"

With that, Fiona stood, slapped Mimi hard across the face, and fled the room.

CHAPTER 18

Isaac watched as the Corvette pulled over and parked in front of him. A blonde woman emerged and walked to the front door of the gallery with keys in hand. He got out of his car and went over to her. "Good morning," he said as he extended his hand. "My name is Isaac Scott. I'm a detective working on the Artimus case."

"Good morning, detective," she replied. She went to switch the keys from her right hand to her left, and they fell to the ground between them. "Oops!" She put a hand to her hip. "I guess I've got the dropsies today," she clucked. As she bent down to retrieve them, her purse slipped from her shoulder and the contents spilled out onto the sidewalk.

Isaac chased after a pen that began rolling toward the street. "Here you go," he said as he handed it to her.

"Oh, thank you." She shoved her wallet into the side pocket. "I'm really not usually this much of a klutz," she declared with a nervous laugh as she scooped the rest of her belongings back into the bag. "There we go." She stood, secured the purse back on her shoulder and reached out her hand to him. "I'm Meredith Stanton, the curator."

He took it. It was shaky. "Nice to meet you, Ms. Stanton."

"Oh please," she said kindly. "Call me Meredith."

Isaac nodded. "Well, nice to meet you, Meredith," he repeated.

She pushed her long ponytail back over her shoulder. "My husband let me know you would be here."

"Please thank him for me, and for meeting me here," Isaac responded.

"Oh look!" Meredith exclaimed and pointed across the street. "There's my assistant Darcy." She waived to her. "Hi Darcy!" she called, trying make it sound like it was the first time they'd seen each other today.

Isaac watched as Darcy emerged from the parking garage on the other side of the road and made her way toward them. She stepped up on the sidewalk next to Meredith.

"Detective, this is Darcy," Meredith said in introduction. "She's here to help me with ah…um….." She stumbled to finish her sentence as she put the key in the lock. "Some …um …."

"Stock," Darcy said.

"Yes, the inventory." She shot Darcy a look of gratitude. "Since the gallery is closed this week, we thought it was a good time." Good, Meredith thought with a sigh of relief. That made sense.

"Nice to meet you, Darcy." Isaac extended his hand. "I'm Isaac Scott."

Darcy nodded and touched his hand lightly. "Uh huh."

Meredith turned the key and held the door open. "Well, now that we're all here, please come in." They stepped inside. "Why don't we go get a nice, cold Arnie Palmer." She smiled at them. "How does that sound? Then you can let us know how we can be of assistance, Detective."

Isaac followed as they wove their way through the gallery past the pedestals holding sculptures and dividing walls that didn't quite reach the ceiling filled with paintings, each individually lit to their best advantage. "You have quite a collection here," Isaac said.

"We do," Meredith agreed. "All created by local artists. Minnesota has an amazing amount of artistic talent."

He paused in front of one of the Artimus paintings done in shades of orange with stokes of a pearly white.

"Stunning, isn't it?" Meredith said.

"Yes," Isaac agreed. "What's it called?"

"Oh, it has no name. Artimus' paintings are numbered in the order they are created."

"Numbered?"

"Yes. We don't want to put a label on these. We let the individual painting speak for itself." She held out her hands, framing the painting. "Some people would say this is a sunset, others might call it fire, and others may see a field of flowers. It's part of the beauty; it can be whatever you want it to be." That was the official line, anyway. He didn't need to know the back story on that, but she would never forget it. It was just after she took control of the gallery.

♦♦♦

Artimus had created three pieces of art for sale and Meredith was completely dumbstruck by how beautiful they were. It was so out of character for the brash, repulsive character she had gotten to know. "What do you call them?" she had asked Art.

He smirked. "These are what you call paintings, doll." He used quotation marks around the word paintings. He shook his head. "Huh. And the jerk Dirk thought a blonde could run this place?"

She took a deep, cleansing breath. "I know they're paintings, Art. But what are their titles?"

"Titles? Again, sweetheart, they're paintings, not books."

She rolled her eyes. "Yes, and paintings have titles. The Mona Lisa, Waterlilies, The Starry Night, to name a few. What titles should I give to these?"

"I don't know, hot stuff, but why don't we go lie down together and think about it?" He winked at her. "I'm sure I could come up with something there."

"Art, stop messing around. If we're going to market these, we'll have to come up with some titles."

"Nah, I'd rather mess around. Don't worry, the jerk won't mind. I saved his life, remember? He owes me."

"That's enough." This was going to be more challenging than she thought. "Enough already. We want to sell these, right? And when someone wants to buy one, we'll need to know which one they are talking about. They'll need to be called something. So Art, let me see if I can help you with this." She pointed to the one on the left. "What was your inspiration for this one?"

"Inspiration?" He let out a laugh. "Money. I want to make money."

"Well good. So do I. So let's try to work together on this." She'd dumb this down a bit. "I mean, what were you *thinking* about when you painted it."

A mischievous grin appeared on his face. "I'll tell you what I was thinking about." His eyes focused in on her cleavage. "I was thinking about your nice, round titties." He reached out his big, bearish hands toward her chest.

She slapped them down. "Stop it."

He nodded at the middle painting. "And for that one, I was thinking about your firm, little ass." He reached around her body with both hands and grasped her cheeks.

She shoved him back. "Stop that!"

"And for that one…" His eyebrows jumped up and down suggestively. "Your…"

"That's enough! Stay away from me." She swatted her hand at him. "Just get out of here!"

He turned and started back toward his lair. "Titties, ass, you-who. I don't care. Name them whatever you want, Doll."

It was after that unpleasant exchange that she enlisted the help of some friends. She had them come by individually and write down what they saw in each of the paintings. Interestingly enough, not one of their impressions or descriptions matched another. That's when she decided to just number the paintings – if for no other reason than to keep track of the inventory. It had been a stroke of genius.

♦ ♦ ♦

"You see, it's all about perceptions. Thus, the name of the gallery." She held her palms to the air and did a little twist back and forth looking like a Barbie doll, then put her hands to her hips. "So, tell me," she said. "What do you see, detective?"

"Hmmm." He took a moment to examine the painting. "I don't know. The color orange is sort of a dichotomy for me. It conjures up warmth, but also anger. A duality of sorts." He turned to look at Meredith. "Something hard to decipher."

The hair stood up on her arms. Somehow that felt personal. "Yes, well then," she said. "Let's get that Arnie Palmer, shall we?"

They all followed her back around the rear wall of the gallery to the break room. Darcy busied herself getting their beverages.

Isaac waited for Meredith to sit, then took a seat of his own. "Before we get started," he said. "I would like to offer my sincere condolences on your loss."

"Yes. It is quite a loss." Meredith bowed her head. "Especially to the art world."

Isaac didn't detect much personal grief in that statement. "Yes, to the art world. That is certain," he agreed. He gestured toward her. "And you as well, I imagine," he said. "How long were you and Artimus acquainted?"

She cocked her head to the left. "It's been about seven years now since we opened the gallery. So, about that long."

Isaac raised his eyebrows. "Seven years!" he exclaimed. "You must have gotten to know him pretty well in that time." He leaned back in his chair. "What can you tell me about him?"

"Well, as you must already know, he was an amazing artist. His paintings are in high demand all over the world."

"Yes, I am aware." Or at least he had become aware since Artimus' death, anyway.

"People would say he was a modern day Van Gogh."

People would say? She seemed reticent to share anything personal about the man. What was that old saying? If you can't say anything nice about someone, don't say anything at all? "We happen to have one of his paintings in our home," he told her, hoping this commonality would help get her to open up a bit.

"You do?" Funny she didn't remember him since she made it a point to keep track of her patrons. "How wonderful. Which one?"

He shook his head. "I really couldn't say. My wife chose it." He smiled. "It's not an original. It's a print. I don't believe we could afford an original."

That explained it. "Oh well, not many can." She smiled a practiced smile. "I appreciate that you appreciate his work."

Darcy set the cold beverages in front of them and took a seat next to Meredith.

"Thank you," Isaac said to her, then returned his attention to Meredith. "So, aside from his artistic acclaim, I'd like to learn more about him as a person."

She sat back in her chair and folded her hands. She exchanged a look with Darcy. "Well, then. How do I describe the great Artimus? Art, we called him." She searched her mind for the right words. Kind words. "He was honest," she said.

Brutally so, Darcy thought to herself.

"He was friendly."

Darcy stifled a laugh. That was a synonym for lecherous she'd never heard before.

"He enjoyed life."

Darcy smirked. Code for "partied a lot."

"You know, it was just an honor to be able to work with him," Meredith said with finality.

"I see. And just how did you come about working together?"

"Well, we owe him such a debt of gratitude. He saved my husband's life."

"He saved your husband's life?" Isaac asked.

"Yes, they were in the service together. Art received the medal of honor for that act of bravery."

So that's how he earned the medal of honor, Isaac thought to himself. Interesting. "I'll look forward to hearing about that when I speak to your husband."

"Oh?" Meredith said.

She looked a bit alarmed, he thought to himself. "Yes, I have an appointment with him tomorrow."

She shifted in her seat. "Dirk didn't mention it," she said, then smiled. "But he's such a busy man, I'm sure it just slipped his mind."

Isaac folded his hands in his lap. "So, Artimus sounds like a stellar individual," he said. A title, in Isaac's opinion, very few individuals would be able to hold. "I must ask, had anything been bothering him lately? Had you noticed any change in his behavior?"

Meredith shook her head. "No, no change in his behavior."

That was certain, Darcy thought to herself.

"Darcy, had you noticed any change in his behavior?" Meredith asked.

"No," Darcy answered.

Isaac took a sip of his Arnie Palmer. Pretty quick responses. Most people would at least give this question *some* consideration before answering. "Does he have any enemies?"

Meredith toyed with a lock of her hair. Probably lots, she thought to herself. "Not that I'm aware of," she lied.

It was clear to Isaac that she was not telling him the whole truth. While trying to appear to be helpful, she was just giving him the whitewash. And, it was also obvious to him, that despite her glowing description, she really didn't care for this man. He could just feel it. He turned his attention to Darcy. She stiffened. "Darcy, do you have anything to add?"

She shook her head. "No. That about covers it."

That about covers it? This was getting him nowhere. He lingered for a moment in case anyone decided to share, but they both sat stock still. "Thank you," he said to them. "Our forensics team will be arriving soon. But before they come in, I'd like to take a look around. Perhaps you can give me a tour?"

"Certainly, Detective. We're happy to do anything we can do to help get this concluded."

Really? Isaac thought to himself.

Meredith began with a tour of the gallery and spent a bit of time talking about each artist. "Their work is vetted and approved. They're here on consignment."

As they spoke, the forensics crew pulled up and started removing their equipment from the van.

Even though she knew they were coming, she looked a bit startled. "I know Dirk gave you the go-ahead to search, but we absolutely can't have anyone touch or disturb any of the artwork. I can't have anything happen to it. It is in our care, and very valuable."

Isaac nodded. "I understand," he said. "When they're ready to come in, I'll direct our team to steer clear from the art." At least this time, he thought to himself. "But it will probably be a little bit before they come inside. I told them to start on the outside of the building."

"The outside?" she said, trying to hide the alarm in her voice. "There's nothing on the outside. Dirk gave you permission to search the gallery." She held out her arms. "This is the gallery."

Interesting reaction. She didn't want him to touch anything in the gallery, but didn't want him to search on the outside either? "Well technically, the property includes both the interior and exterior," he told her, then smiled kindly. "It's just standard procedure."

She wrung her hands together. "Yes, of course. Standard procedure. It's just that there's just nothing out there." She forced a smile and a little laugh. "Except maybe some garbage that has blown in."

Isaac now knew that one of the very first things he'd want to see after this search was just exactly what was found in the dumpster. "So you were saying that the artists' works are here on consignment," he said to Meredith. "Was that true of Artimus' paintings as well?"

"Oh no. The gallery owns all that Artimus created. Art would get a percentage when his works sold."

"Really." That was certainly reason enough to keep the memory of Artimus unscathed.

"Yes, this gallery was purchased by Dirk's parents so that Artimus could display and sell his work, in gratitude for his saving their son's life. But, of course, there are numerous expenses that go along with it - maintenance costs, utility costs, advertising costs, employee's wages, event expenses — you name it. They wanted to be sure that those costs would be covered going forward. It was quite generous of them, but they also had very good business sense."

"Indeed."

She then took him into a large, dark room that was the area Isaac had noticed from the outside with the black-out shades. "This is where we store Artimus' paintings."

There were hundreds of them. All the same shape. All the same size. "My, my, he was industrious."

"Yes, and even though Artimus would create several new paintings monthly, we only introduce ten or so at a time. We don't want to glut the market so that the paintings will hold their value. Sadly, these will be the last of them. We store them in the dark, temperature controlled, humidity-controlled room so that there's no color degradation."

It was quite impressive. But he still had yet to see where all of these were created. "Where does Artimus paint?"

"Art occupied the lower level. No one was permitted to go down there. He insisted on complete privacy when he was creating."

Finally. Isaac hoped that this would be where he would find the elusive pills and answer Cynthia's question as to where the TCA's that were in Artimus' system came from. "Please show it to me."

"Certainly. Give me just a minute and I will get the key." Meredith disappeared into her office. She could hear clanging out the back of the building. What were they doing out there? She could feel her body temperature rising. Everything she'd worked so hard to get rid of was in that dumpster. She took some deep breaths. All the pornography, the liquor bottles – that was all there. But the most concerning was the rest. She ran her hands over her head. Who could possibly make the connection between that and Artimus' work? Probably no one, she assured herself. She took another deep breath. *What had Dirk been thinking?*

Isaac and Darcy stood by the doorway to the basement waiting for Meredith's return.

"Have you been working at the gallery a long time?"

"A few months," she said. "I came here from a gallery in New York."

New York? She didn't sound like a New Yorker. "Oh. Is that where you're from?"

But before she could answer, Meredith returned. She turned her attention to Darcy. "Darcy, please stay here and don't let the police in until we are back."

Meredith and Isaac descended the stairs to the basement into a large room with a fully stocked bar at one end and a couch against the neighboring wall. A large screen TV hung on the wall directly across from the couch. Isaac walked about the room taking it all in. He noticed some deep, square indentations in the newly vacuumed carpet, where something heavy must have been sitting. It looked like whatever it was, had been very recently removed. He stood in the middle of the rectangular shape made by the base of whatever it was and took a turn around. On the wall directly across were some nails in the wall. He walked towards them. Small splatters of paint dotted the floor beneath the nails. "Was this where he painted?" he asked Meredith.

"Yes, I believe so." She knew so, but didn't want to share how she happened upon that information.

Isaac walked down a hallway to the right of the bar with Meredith following closely behind. He entered the bathroom keeping his fingers crossed, hoping he would find the antidepressant pills, or at least their container. He opened the cabinet above the sink. Inside he found the usual stuff, aspirin, ibuprofen and other standard medicines, but no prescription bottles. Isaac sighed. There was still the slightest amount of hope that the pills were intentionally hidden in one of these other bottles for one reason or another. If they were, the forensics team would certainly find them.

"It's very clean," Isaac commented. Like it was just cleaned yesterday, he thought to himself. Nothing was a bit dusty or out of place. He turned toward Meredith. "Did his sister clean for him?"

She looked confused. "What?"

"Did Artimus' sister clean for him?" Isaac repeated. "I know she took care of his home, I was wondering if she also cleaned for him here."

Meredith looked at him wide-eyed. "Art has a sister?"

CHAPTER 19

Fiona burst through her hotel room door and fell face down on the bed, tears streaming down her cheeks. She let out a large sob and rolled over. She stared at the ceiling. Could it be true? Did her father kill her mother? No. No. She couldn't believe that. She didn't believe that. She wouldn't believe that. But that one day…. That day the police were there….

◆ ◆ ◆

Her mother had been gone for three months by that time, and it was clear she'd have to fend for herself. Fend for herself *and* take care of their home. Her father busied himself with the work on the farm and didn't say much anymore. Art begrudgingly helped out when he wasn't practicing with his football team.

All the same, she was used to having chores. Everyone had to pitch in on the farm. She had always been expected to help her mother in the kitchen, help keep the house clean, and repair their clothing. So, at eight years old, she was capable of many things.

She had been on the swing when they arrived.

She saw her father come out of the barn. "Go to your room," he yelled out to her.

She dragged her feet to stop the swing and watched as the policemen got out of the car. They walked over to her father.

He looked over his shoulder at her. "Go to your room, damn it!" he hollered.

She got off the swing and walked slowly toward the house, keeping her eyes on him. The police showed her father some papers. She could tell he wasn't happy. She wasn't sure what he said, but he threw up his arms and shook his head wildly.

The police were there for hours. As instructed, she stayed in her room, but with her ear to the door. She could hear the shuffling of feet, the opening and closing of closets, drawers and cupboards and muffled voices.

After they left, she came out of her room and found her father at the kitchen table with his head in his hands.

"What were they looking for, daddy?" she asked him.

He looked up with angry eyes. "Rats. They were looking for rats. You know we have a bad rat problem here. A really bad rat problem. Right? If anyone asks you about it, you tell them. We have a really bad rat problem at the farm."

She knew better than to contradict her father when he was cross, so she left it alone. And from then on, he left her alone.

That's when she started painting the flowers on her wall. She painted every chance she got until it was completely covered. Her own private garden.

♦ ♦ ♦

Vick entered the hotel as the camera crew packed up their van. He walked up to the front desk. "Was that Mimi Winslow?" he asked Patience.

"Yes." She looked at him with wide eyes. "Are you here to arrest her?" she asked in a panic.

"Mimi Winslow?" he asked.

"No." She chewed nervously on a cuticle. "Fiona. Fiona Farkus."

He laughed. "Arrest her? No, I have an appointment with her."

"An appointment?"

Vick frowned then pointed over his shoulder toward the door. "Did something just happen here?"

"Oh yes," Patience confirmed. "It sure did."

"Fill me in."

She rubbed her temples. "Oh, it was bad," she said. "Mimi accused Fiona of murdering Artimus."

"Mimi accused Fiona of murder?" he repeated with astonishment.

"Yes. Can you imagine?" She put her hands to her cheeks. "A murderer staying in our hotel," she moaned.

Vick ran his hand over his hair. Damn that Mimi! Always sticking her nose into everything. This was not going to go over well with Petruco if a reporter discovered the murderer before the police did.

Patience raised her brows. "And then Fiona slapped her."

"Fiona slapped Mimi?"

"Yes! She slapped *Mimi Winslow.*" She said the name like Mimi was the Queen of England.

Huh. Good for Fiona, Vick thought to himself. "Where is she now?"

"Fiona?"

Vick nodded slowly. "Yes, Fiona," he said like Patience was denser than a brick. "The one I'm here to see."

"She's in her room."

"Would you please call her and let her know Detective Marchese is here for our meeting?"

Patience dialed the room number. It rang and rang. "No one's answering," she said.

"What's the room number?"

♦♦♦

Vick went up to the third floor and knocked on the door. "Fiona, it's Detective Marchese. I'm here for our meeting."

He heard her voice through the door. "Are you going to arrest me?" she asked.

"Arrest you? No. We had a meeting scheduled, remember?"

The door slowly opened, and she looked up at him, her face moist from the tears. "Hold me, Detective," she cried, then leaned her body onto his and buried her face in his chest.

"Hey! Hey! Hey! Not on the shirt!" He pushed her back and looked down at his shirt. Smudges of black, pink and green were left behind. "Shit," he said under his breath. He looked up and down the hallway to be sure no one was watching. "Let's go into your room." He pushed her inside and sat her on the bed. "Stay there," he instructed, then made a beeline for the bathroom.

"Mimi Winslow was here," she told him.

Vick wetted a towel and started dabbing the stains. "Yeah, I saw her leaving," he said as he came around the corner from the sink.

"She said my dad killed my mom."

"Really?" He hadn't heard that. "Did he?" he said, as he wiped some more.

"She said that's why he killed himself."

"He killed himself?" he repeated, pretending he was listening. He ducked back into the bathroom and added some soap.

"How could she know that?"

"You got me. But she's got some good researchers there at the television station." This wouldn't be the first time Mimi came up with information before the police did. "Shit!" he exclaimed. "This isn't coming out!"

"I don't believe her. Nobody ever told me that."

"Right. She makes stuff up all the time." That was true too. She was often known to twist the facts and report conjectures as truth. "Do you have any Spray 'n Wash?"

"No. She does?"

He picked up the phone and dialed the desk. "Yeah, that's what reporters do," he said to Fiona. Patience answered the phone. "Can you send up some Spray 'n Wash or Shout - some kind of stain remover?" he asked her.

"Stain remover?" Patience said with alarm.

"Yeah. And hurry," Vick said and hung up the phone.

"And then she accused me of killing Art," Fiona said.

Vick looked in the mirror and then at Fiona. "You know this shirt cost two hundred dollars."

She slammed her hands down on the bed. "Are you listening to me? Fuck the shirt. I'll buy you ten more."

She grabbed the satchel at the side of the bed, pulled out a wad of cash, and shook it at him. "Here take the money!" she yelled, just as a knock came on the door.

"I've got the stain cleaner," they heard the manager, Duncan, call through the door.

Vick pointed a finger at Fiona. "Stay put," he said, then opened the door.

"Everything all right in there?" Duncan asked.

Vick reached out and took the cleaner from his hand. "Everything's fine," he said as he closed the door in Duncan's face.

Fiona threw the wad at Vick. "Did you hear me?"

"Where did you get that money?"

"Forget the money! I *said* she accused me of killing Art!"

"Yeah, I heard that part."

She looked up at him. "You gotta help me," she pleaded.

"Okay. Okay. You know, just calm down," he said trying to console her, this skill being way out of his comfort zone. "Let's go through this." He spritzed a bit of the cleaner on his shirt. "So, where were you that night?"

"At the Varsity Theatre to see the Rubber Bandits concert."

"So you went with friends?"

"No. I was alone."

"Did anybody see you there?"

"The place was packed. A gazillion people saw me there."

"Anybody in particular? Someone who could vouch that you were there?"

She shrugged. "Not really."

"How late were you there?"

"I don't know. 'Till after the band was done and then some."

Hopefully the Varsity Theatre had good security cameras that would confirm she was there, he thought to himself. "Well, there you go." He smiled at her. "You have an alibi. No matter what Mimi said. She's just trying to get the big scoop. She likes to be outrageous. It helps with ratings."

"She's a bitch."

"Yes, she is," he agreed. He lifted his brows then gave her a wink. "But in reality, she's just jealous of you."

"You think so?"

"Sure, you've just inherited a fortune and ah…" He couldn't believe he was saying this. "Have a cool new clothing line."

"You think so?"

"Sure, I get this kind of thing all the time. I know people like Mimi. I mean, you know." He smoothed the hair back over his head and checked his look in the mirror. "Some people might say I'm vain, but they're just jealous."

She nodded admiringly.

"Sure, they're just wishing they were me. It's the same with Mimi. And ha! She doesn't know it, but she just gave you headlines. Bigger headlines than she'll get."

She smiled. "You think so?"

"Of course. You know what they say, bad press is better than no press. And in all cases, it's better than boring good press."

Her eyes lit up. "You think so?"

"Sure. Now where did you get that money?"

CHAPTER 20

Vick entered the room with his arms raised high over his head like he just scored the winning touchdown. "Oh yeah," he said. "I've got some great intel."

Isaac chuckled. "Are you expecting applause?"

"Always." He grinned and dropped into the seat across the table. "You'll never guess what happened at the Bayview Inn today."

"The Bayview Inn?"

"Yeah, that's where Fiona Farkus is staying. Nice place. Right on the lake."

"So, tell me. What happened?"

"Fiona had an interview with Mimi Winslow this morning which is why she couldn't meet with me earlier. And, *get this*, Mimi accused Fiona of killing Artimus."

"She what?"

"See, I told you you wouldn't believe it. But Mimi's got it all wrong," he said with a smirk.

Isaac furrowed his brow as questions flooded his head. "She has it wrong? How do you know that? And why does Mimi think Fiona killed him? Please Vick, do explain."

"I guess Mimi said something about Fiona's dad killing her mom or something like that and then accused Fiona of doing the same to her brother."

Isaac scratched his head. "That's it? Did Mimi offer any other evidence?"

He shrugged. "That's all Fiona told me. We'll have to watch the broadcast to find out."

"That's kind of important information, Vick."

Vick ran his hands over his head, smoothing his perfectly coifed hair. "Well, Isaac, she can't have any proof because Fiona has an alibi."

"She does?" That *was* good intel. "Nice work," he commended. "Now back up a bit. I want the whole story."

"Sure. It's a good one. So I show up for my interview with Fiona and see the Channel 9 News van loading up and Mimi Winslow getting into a car. She even waved at me. Had a big smile on her face. Anyway, I go in and don't see

Fiona in the lobby, so I go up to the desk clerk. She tells me about the interview and says that Fiona slapped Mimi." He slapped the table and let out a belly laugh.

Just then, the door to the meeting room burst open and they looked up to see Petruco with a big scowl on his face.

"What's so damn funny?" he asked. "Don't you know we're investigating a murder here?"

"Fiona Farkus slapped Mimi Winslow!" Vick told him. "Can you believe it? She slapped her!" he repeated.

Petruco let out a snort. "Slapped Winslow?"

"I've always wanted to do that," Vick added.

"Me too," Petruco agreed, then looked momentarily confused. "*Who* slapped her?" he asked.

"Fiona Farkus. Artimus' sister. During their interview." Vick looked at his smart watch. "It's airing at five o'clock."

The smile disappeared from Petruco's face. "An interview with Mimi Winslow?" That was never good news. "Shit," he said under his breath.

"Okay. We've got an hour until it comes on," Isaac said.

Petruco started pacing back and forth across the room, with his shoulders hunched and his head held low in his signature vulture stance.

"Tell us about what happened during your interview with Fiona," Isaac said to Vick. "What's her alibi?"

"She says she was at the Varsity Theatre that night to see the Rubber Bandits," Vick told them. "Good band. Phenomenal guitarist." He looked toward the ceiling. "Will somebody." He crinkled his nose. "Will Robinson? No, no, that's from that old TV show…."

"So, she was with this guitarist?" Isaac asked.

"Oh, no. She was just there to see the band."

"So, she was with friends that can confirm that?"

"Oh no. She was alone."

"But you believe her because…?"

Vick shrugged. "I don't know."

Isaac sighed. Vick wasn't the best at reading character. "You know she could have made that up. We'll need substantiation."

Vick squawked. "That's easy, Mr. skeptical. We just check the security cameras."

Petruco stopped his pacing. "We'll need a warrant for that."

"She's definitely a top suspect," Isaac told him. "She was the one who found the body, she also cleaned the house just prior to that getting rid of any evidence, and she stands to inherit millions. Will that be enough?"

Petruco nodded like a pecking bird. "I'll talk to the judge." He made his way to the door.

"Make sure you're back by five o'clock," Vick called after him. "You won't want to miss this!" He sat back in his chair and wrapped his hands across the back of his head, elbows sticking out to the sides. "It will be so satisfying to prove Mimi wrong."

Isaac rubbed his forehead. Vick could be so arrogant. And that arrogance oftentimes interfered with his job performance. Finding Fiona in a crowd at the Varsity Theatre may not be so easy. It was like Finding Waldo with the images constantly changing and moving across the page. "Did you go through that list of questions I gave you with Fiona?"

"Well, you know, most of them." He dropped his arms and leaned forward. "You're going to like this. I found out about the money that Artimus had hidden all over his house."

"Oh?" That *was* good news.

"Fiona said Art didn't trust banks since the bank repossessed their father's farm. He didn't trust lawyers either. He blamed them and their exorbitant fees for his father's inability to pay the mortgage, so I doubt we'll find any will."

No will? That's convenient for Fiona being Artimus' sole beneficiary, Isaac thought to himself. "Did she have any insight into Artimus' state of mind? Had he been depressed lately?" Isaac asked. Or most importantly, he thought to himself, "Was he taking any antidepressants?"

"We didn't get to that."

"Vick," Isaac said with reproach. "This is important stuff. Especially if she's not the culprit, we'll need to look elsewhere. Does she know if he had any enemies that would like to cause him harm?"

"Look, Isaac," Vick countered. "She was in a state of distress. I couldn't ask her those kind of things just then. But I've got another meeting scheduled with her tomorrow. I'll ask her then."

"Okay. I guess that makes sense," Isaac said. It wasn't uncommon for those experiencing grief to be unable to focus on anything other than their grief. At least Vick had the wherewithal to schedule another meeting. "This time, make sure you address the questions. Tell her we need any information she has that could assist us in solving the case. If she's innocent, she should want to help."

"Well, okay *boss*." Vick rolled his eyes. "But Isaac, as she told us at the scene, she thinks he got drunk, fell into the pool, and drowned. He can't swim, remember?"

"Seems like you're getting a little defensive about this, Vick. Take a step back. Remember, we're investigating this as a murder. Don't forget that."

◆ ◆ ◆

Petruco returned just minutes before five o'clock. "Got it," he told them, referring to the search warrant. "Peg's sending a uniform over to serve it." He pulled up a chair next to Isaac.

Isaac switched on the television.

They all watched as Mimi appeared with a prominent pink welt on her left cheek. Nothing had been done to try to cover it up with make-up, in fact it seemed like, if anything, it had been enhanced. She introduced the interview, and the tape began to roll. Fiona's clothing creations hung in the background, but Fiona's sales pitch had been edited out. The camera zoomed in on Fiona as Mimi recounted her family history and drilled her with questions. It was hard to watch. Fiona had been completely blindsided, and Mimi had taken full advantage.

When Mimi waved around the report showing Artimus had large amounts of anti-depressants in his system, Petruco stood and shouted, "Where did she get that information?"

Isaac grimaced, wondering exactly the same thing.

"Fiona didn't mention anything about that when I talked to her," Vick said.

Petruco looked down and practically growled at him.

"The Examiner's report isn't completed yet, Captain," Isaac told Petruco. "What she's saying is pure conjecture at this point." And Cynthia Chu was going to be steaming mad about this leak in her department, he didn't add.

Then the scene on the screen changed, and a photo of Vick with Fiona in his arms at the door of her hotel room filled the screen.

All their mouths dropped open.

They couldn't believe their eyes when footage of Vick talking with a Channel 9 reporter outside the station followed. "There's been talk that Fiona Farkus was responsible for the murder of her brother, Artimus," the reporter said to him. "What can you tell us about this Detective Marchese?"

"That's just false," Vick told him. "Fiona Farkus has an alibi for the evening."

Mimi Winslow came back on camera with the photo of Vick and Fiona prominently displayed in the background. "Just what is this alibi, Detective Marchese? Or perhaps there is some collusion happening here? I'll leave it up to the viewers to decide." She winked at the camera. "Mimi Winslow, at your service."

Isaac turned off the television and leaned back in his chair.

Petruco narrowed his hawk eyes and zeroed in on Vick. "You're off the case." Then he turned his attention to Isaac. "Where's Detective Bryant?"

"He'll be back next week."

"Not acceptable. Get him back here. Now!"

CHAPTER 21

Claudia met Isaac at the door. She'd been pacing there for what seemed like hours waiting for his return home. "I saw the interview," she told him.

"I think the whole world saw the interview," he responded.

She took him in her arms. "Mimi was ruthless. That poor child."

Isaac nuzzled his head in her neck. Nothing was more comforting than holding his wife. He looked over at the picture hanging over their loveseat. "I've never seen Petruco so manic. The whole department is on edge."

"Because of Vick?"

He nodded. "Vick's off the case. I imagine he'll be fired over this." He released her and made his way to the kitchen. He pulled out a glass and filled it with water. "He says it was all innocent. He said that she leaned into him and got make up all over his shirt. That he just went into her hotel room to wash it off." He shook his head. "You know how vain he is."

"You believe him?"

He turned and leaned back against the counter. "Yeah. But that won't matter."

She let out a long breath. "What was he thinking?"

Isaac grunted. "He wasn't."

She leaned back against the counter next to him. "Is it true Fiona Farkus has an alibi? That would be helpful, wouldn't it?"

"That certainly would be helpful," he agreed. "We're checking it out, but it's going to take a while. In the meantime, the press is all over this. Petruco is sputtering banalities and refusing to answer questions. It's very unlike him. He's in a tough place."

"That's got to be hard on you."

He shrugged. "Nothing to do about it but try to move forward." He took a sip of water. "Where are the kids?"

"Honey, it's ten o'clock; they've gone off to bed."

"Right." He gave her a squeeze. "You should too."

She reached up and gently held his head in her hands. "What about you? You need a good rest after such a long day."

"Nah. I'm going to go read some reports here where it's nice and quiet."

"Okay." She gave him a kiss on the lips. "But don't stay up too late."

♦♦♦

Isaac went into his office, opened his backpack and took out the initial report from the search of the gallery. To his dismay, no prescription bottles were found in the dumpster or anywhere in Artimus' basement space. The analysis of the pills in the medicine cabinet was not yet complete, but he was becoming less and less optimistic they would find them there either. So where did they come from?

Due to Ms. Stanton's reaction when told about the outside search, he felt that there had to be something there she did not want discovered. Was whatever it was related to the murder? Or was it something else? Whatever it was, Isaac knew he had to find it. He began to examine the photos of what they had retrieved and laid them out across his desk. The top layer was just as he had remembered. Porn magazines, empty liquor bottles and beer cans, and boxes of floor tiles of various kinds. Strips of plastic, evenly cut as though put through a shredder, were littered around the rest. A bit lower in the dumpster were some twisted and broken art canvas' that looked to be the same size and shape as Artimus' other paintings, shredded paper and some fashion magazines.

He sat and stared at the photos until his head hurt' waiting for that revelation, that ah-ha moment when it all made sense. But nothing came to him. Not the slightest inkling of an idea, not even a hunch.

Perhaps he was just too tired. He hoped a good night's sleep would give him new insight. He shut off the office light and started up the stairs when he heard his daughter Avery call out to him.

"Help Daddy! Help!" she yelled.

He hurried to her room. She was sitting up in her bed, but still half asleep. His heart sank. More night terrors. He sat next to her and took her in his arms. She leaned into him and started to cry.

He stroked her hair while the tears subsided.

She sat back and wiped her face. "How do you do it, daddy?" she asked. "How do you see dead bodies all the time and not have nightmares?"

Of course, she was talking about the badly decomposed dead body she fell on while trying to escape the groping hands of the hormone-crazed young boy who lured her back into the woods last spring. Without a doubt, it was one of the most gruesome corpses Isaac had run across in his career.

"I just can't get the sight of that out of my head," she said. A shiver ran up her spine.

He thought about it for a minute. It certainly was the hardest thing about being a homicide detective. Seeing all the murder victims and having to be a witness to the viciousness of those that killed them made it hard not to lose faith in the human race. It often did cause him nightmares, but he'd learned to cope with the fact that it was an element of the job. Which then begged the question, just what was it that kept him in this profession? The answer was actually quite easy. There was no doubt about it. It was the catching of the culprits that spurred him on.

"I guess I just know that, some how, some way, I will find the guilty person," Isaac told her. "So I can give closure to the victim's family. That's what drives me and helps me get through. Bringing good out of bad," he told her. But he also knew that sugar-coating this would never help her truly heal. He knew he had to be completely honest with her. It couldn't just be swept under the rug. It was something she'd have to deal with head on. "But I have nightmares too," he admitted. He took her hands in his. "And I can't tell you that this won't resurface again, but I can assure you that I understand what you're going through and that I'm always here for you."

She pulled her hands away from his and put them to her temples. "I did this all to myself you know. I went into the woods with that boy even though I knew I shouldn't have." She crossed her arms over her chest. "And this is the price I pay for being bad."

"Oh no, honey." He leaned in and put his arm around her shoulders. "You can't beat yourself up like that."

"But if I hadn't done that. None of this would have happened."

He pulled her in close. "We all make decisions every day and they all have their consequences. Sometimes good, sometimes bad. But we can't beat ourselves up when things don't go the way we expect them to. We just need to learn from them. Maybe it's not so pleasant at the time, but it's effective. Those experiences will make us a better, stronger, smarter person." He kissed her on the top of her head, then sat back and smiled. "I'm going to tell you a story about when you were just a tiny little toddler."

She moved back on the bed and crossed her legs.

"You were so curious and wanted to explore everything," Isaac began. "And at that age, everything – and I mean *everything* - went into your mouth. So one day, I turned just in time to see you snatch half a lemon off the table. You put it towards your mouth with a sneaky little grin on your face. I called out no, no, Avery, too sour! But you didn't listen and took a big bite into it. You should have seen your face! Your mouth puckered up, your cheeks sucked in and your eyes got as big as saucers!" He chuckled. "I couldn't help but laugh at the sight."

The corners of her mouth turned up just a bit.

He sat back next to her on the bed. "You know, you learned something that day. You learned that lemons are sour - and I'm sure you've never forgotten that lesson. So, we need to start viewing this from a different perspective. Instead of kicking yourself over and over, let's look at all you've learned." He pulled the blanket up and covered up her legs. "First, I'm confident that you will make better choices in situations like these in the future."

She hung her head and nodded shamefacedly.

He took his hand and lifted her chin. He looked into her sad, brown eyes. "No, sweetheart. No. Hold your head high. You've learned an important lesson and you are stronger for it. Right?"

"I guess so," she said half-heartedly.

"You are. I want you to internalize that. Make it a part of who you are."

She sat a bit straighter. "Okay."

"As far as the dead body is concerned, that was pure accident – and actually, quite fortuitous."

She cocked her head to the side. "What does fortuitous mean?"

"It means a lucky accident."

She shook her head. "It sure didn't feel lucky to me."

"But if you hadn't discovered the body, it might never have been found."

"I know." She scrunched up her face. "And Edna knew him," she said. "How weird is that?"

"Yes, she did. He was the missing husband of her former employer, Crystal."

"Of Crystal's Palace."

"Yes. And your discovery allowed Edna to take the balance of Crystal's estate and invest it in Crystal's Palace which is helping hundreds of families."

"Yeah."

"If you hadn't found the body, that may never have happened."

"That's good, right?"

He smiled. "That's very good." He kissed her on the forehead. "And it helped me close out a file that I had been working on for three months. So you see, all kinds of good has come out of this bad." He reached out his arms for her. "Let's focus on that."

She leaned in and rested her head on his chest. "Daddy, I don't want to go to see my counselor anymore. I've talked to her about this enough. It isn't helping any-more." She looked up at him with her deep brown, inno-cent eyes. "I'd rather talk to you about it. You know what it's like and can relate to me. Is that okay?"

He hugged her close. "Of course, honey. I'm happy to talk with you anytime."

"Thanks, daddy. I feel safe in your arms."

He rested his head on hers. Tears came to his eyes. How could one feel so sad and happy at the same time?

CHAPTER 22

Isaac pulled up and parked in front of *Perceptions*. It was indeed a fitting name for the gallery. It was so true that what you see depends on how you look at it. Each person's point of view is continually developed and refined by their own personal experiences. Our perspectives are constructed of the beliefs and the emotions we internalize from those experiences. As some smart person once said, we don't see things how they are, we see them as we are.

That being said, Isaac was still having trouble getting a bead on this man Artimus. How could he reconcile the

Artimus who appeared to be a drunk womanizer with the Artimus who painted beautiful paintings like the one Claudia chose to hang over their loveseat, and who donated those valuable paintings to good causes such as Crystal's Palace? He was hoping his interview with the man whose life Artimus saved, Dirk Stanton, would help.

Meredith met him at the door. "Good morning, Detective."

"Good morning."

She locked the door behind him. "Dirk's in my office. Please follow me."

They wove their way through the pedestals and separating walls to her office at the back of the gallery opposite the café area where they had been the last time he visited. Isaac followed her inside.

The man behind the desk stood. He had a head full of sandy colored hair, broad shoulders, and looked like he came from money.

"Detective Scott, this is my husband Dirk," Meredith said.

Isaac held out his hand.

"Dirk, this is Detective Scott," she said completing the introduction.

Dirk took Isaac's hand. "Nice to meet you Detective. Please take a seat." He gestured to the chair across from him.

Isaac did as he suggested.

"May I get you a cup of coffee? An Arnie Palmer, perhaps?" Meredith asked.

"No, thank you," Isaac responded politely.

"Well, then," Meredith said. "I'll just take a seat." She walked over and pulled up a chair next to her husband. She looked up with a nervous sort of smile. "How's the investigation going, Detective?" she asked.

He smiled his most understanding smile. "I imagine you're concerned, being how close you all must have been. But all I can say is that it's ongoing."

"What about this supposed sister of his? Has that been confirmed? Because we never heard he had a sister. I don't know why he would keep that from us."

"Don't be silly, Meredith," Dirk interjected. "Art didn't ever talk about *any* family." He looked at Isaac. "Quite frankly, we didn't care enough to ask about his family either."

Meredith slapped at his arm. "Dirk, you don't really mean that." She smiled at Isaac. "He doesn't really mean that."

Dirk shrugged.

Interesting. "Mr. Stanton, I'd like to find out more about Artimus on a personal level," Isaac said. "Do you know if he suffered from depression now or at any time in his life?"

"No need to be so formal, Detective, around here we call Artimus, Art," Dirk said.

Isaac nodded in affirmation.

"The only time I've ever seen Art looked depressed is when he lost a bet." Dirk rubbed his chin thinking about it. "No," he backtracked. "That wasn't really depressed, it was more like angry."

"Was he a gambler?"

"Not any more than any of the other soldiers. It was a way to pass time and think about something other than snipers and land mines."

"Yes, I heard you were in Afghanistan together. I understand that Artimus, I mean Art," Isaac corrected himself. "Saved your life. Is that so?"

"That's what I'm told," Dirk said. "I was unconscious at the time." To Dirk, the idea of Art ever saving another's life, and in particular his, was absurd.

♦ ♦ ♦

Still, according to all accounts, Art had saved Dirk's life. Dirk didn't remember all that transpired after their jeep was hit by sniper fire and they jumped out and took positions behind the vehicle - just that there was an explosion right in front of him and then he blacked out. From Art's account, Dirk was injured by that explosion, so Art picked him up and valiantly carried him in his arms to safety. For this, Art received the medal of honor from the United States Government and the everlasting gratitude of Dirk's wealthy parents for saving their son's life.

But Dirk knew, deep in his heart, that this was no valiant rescue. Art was just using Dirk's body as a shield for protection so that Art, himself, didn't get hit while he ran cowardly from the fight. Dirk was certain of this because of the bullets that were lodged in the back of his spine. There was no other explanation as to how they got there. Art's account of carrying Dirk in his arms to safety just didn't hold water. But on the other hand, Art hiding underneath Dirk's body while running from the battle, now that made sense.

When Dirk's parents insisted on showing their appreciation to Art for saving their only child's life, all were surprised to hear that Art, of all people, wanted to paint. Not the interior and/or exterior of homes, but create works of art. When Dirk heard this, he just figured it was another one of Art's ludicrous jokes. He could hear him say "Yeah, my name's Art and I make art." But, much to Dirk's surprise, Art actually produced a nice-looking painting. So, Dirk's parents purchased the building in the Uptown neighborhood of Minneapolis and granted Art use of the space to produce and show his art. Against Dirk's strong objections, Dirk's parents also insisted that Dirk run the gallery. After all, they said, Dirk should be grateful to Art; he owed Art his life.

But just the sight of Art made Dirk ill, so Meredith stepped in and took charge - and did so with gusto. Meredith changed the name of the gallery from '*Art by Art*' to '*Perceptions*,' increased the selling price of his paintings from fifty dollars to five thousand dollars, and did a complete remodel of the space, transforming the entire atmosphere.

Thus, Art created his paintings in his dark, basement cave, and Meredith managed the gallery. And through Meredith's fabulous marketing, Artimus' paintings and the gallery soon became renowned.

♦♦♦

"So you don't believe that he saved your life?" Isaac asked.

"Well, he carried me to safety, but I believe it was done more to save Art's life than mine." There, he'd said it aloud and it felt like a weight had been lifted from his chest. All these years of having to glorify this vile man just to sell his paintings had taken a toll.

Meredith gasped. "Honey, you don't really mean that." She looked at Isaac. "We are very grateful that Art saved Dirk's life."

"Yes, true," Dirk agreed. "Even if I was just used as a human shield."

Isaac nodded. He was liking this man. No pretenses. He was telling it as he saw it. That was very rare in Isaac's line of work. "I commend your honesty, Mr. Stanton. What more can you tell me about Mr. Farkus."

Dirk smiled, happy for the opportunity to finally share the truth. "He was crass, vulgar and uneducated. He liked women. He used women. I don't believe he cared about anyone other than himself." He sat back in his seat. "There you have it. The honest truth about the brilliant artist, Artimus."

"So I'm getting the impression you didn't care for this man, Artimus, is that correct?"

"That would be correct."

"Would you go so far to say you hated him?"

"Detective, hate wouldn't be a strong enough word for how much I disliked Arty Farkus."

Meredith put her hand on her husband's shoulder. "You must understand, Detective. Artimus was an artist. Oftentimes ones with great talent are eccentric, and Art was no exception," she said trying to put a good face on it. "I hope our comments will be kept strictly confidential."

"I will not be sharing this information with the press, if that's what you are concerned about," Isaac assured her.

"Good." Meredith pressed her lips together. "I'm not sure how to say this politely, so I'll be frank. Art liked to drink."

"I see."

"Honestly, my guess would be that he drank too much that night, fell into his pool and drown. You know, he can't swim."

"Yes. I have heard that. But I hope you understand that we will need to explore all possibilities until we have proof of that."

She fidgeted with the beads of her bracelet. "Well, of course," she agreed tentatively. "I mean, especially with such a well-known person," she conceded. "Sure."

Dirk raised his right hand. "I can confirm that he was very drunk that night," he volunteered.

Meredith's eyes turned to saucers. "What?!"

"I stopped over that night to confront him about a large withdrawal from the gallery account," Dirk said.

"You were there?" Meredith exclaimed.

"Yes," he confirmed.

"You didn't tell me that."

"I guess it slipped my mind," he said to her. He turned his attention back to Isaac. "Art was back by the pool. He looked completely wasted. I asked him about the withdrawal, and he just sat there and stared at me."

"About what time were you there?" Isaac asked.

"It was just after seven o'clock. I know this because I stopped to pick up my dry cleaning at Pilgrim Dry Cleaners just before, and they closed at seven."

Isaac pulled out his note pad and jotted down the time. "Can you tell me more about his condition at that time?"

"Sure. He was practically catatonic. I was almost yelling at him, but he wouldn't say a word. He didn't move a muscle. Just sat there smirking that obnoxious smirk."

"I see. So what did you do?"

"I slapped him."

Meredith gasped.

Isaac made a point not to react. "And what did he do then?"

"Nothing. The jackass. He just sat there. Trying to get my goat."

"And did he?"

"Yes, of course. He always does."

"So what did you do then?"

"I stormed out." Dirk shook his head in disgust. "He always knew how to torment me. It's what he enjoyed most in the world, it would seem." He folded his hands in his lap. "I'm so glad he's gone."

Isaac's brows went up.

Meredith took Dirk by the chin. "You don't mean that, honey," she said. She looked at Isaac. "He doesn't mean that."

Dirk swatted her hand away. "Oh yes I do," Dirk said.

"Mr. Stanton, did you want him gone enough to aid in his demise?" Isaac asked.

Dirk grunted. "If you're asking if I killed him, Detective, I did not. I imagine he finally got up out of his chair and fell into the pool just like Meredith said. I'm just saying that I'm not unhappy about it."

CHAPTER 23

Isaac opened the door of his car and watched the steam billow out. He gingerly slipped his foot inside and managed to push on the brake just enough to be able to start the car without sitting on the hot leather. He'd let the air conditioning cycle out some of the heat for a few minutes before getting in himself.

As he shut the door to the vehicle, his cell phone rang. It wasn't a number he recognized, but that wasn't unusual on his work cell. He handed out his business card to any number of people who may be of assistance on his cases. "Detective Scott, speaking," he answered.

"Detective, this is Darcy from the gallery. I have some information regarding Artimus. Do you have a minute to talk with me?"

Information she had been reticent to divulge in front of Meredith? he wondered. "Certainly. Can you come down to the station this afternoon?"

"Well no, I was hoping we could talk at the gallery."

"Sure. That would be fine. I just happen to be there now."

"I know," she interrupted. "I'm in the parking garage across the street."

She was watching him? "Okay." He looked across the street. "Well, by all means, please come on over."

"No," she said. "I can't. We have to wait until after Meredith and Dirk leave." She paused for a moment. "It involves them."

"Oh?" Interesting. "Okay. Then I'll just wait here."

"No," she said again. "You can't do that. They won't leave until they think you're gone."

"So, you want me to go drive around the block or something?"

"Yes. Drive away. I'll call you once they leave."

He really didn't want to spend an afternoon driving around waiting for them to go. "Do you think they will be leaving soon?"

"Yes," she affirmed. "Like I said, they're just waiting for *you* to go."

"Really?" How mysterious. "Okay." He got in his still sweltering car, buckled his seat belt, and put the car in drive. "I'm off," he said.

"Good. I'll let you know when the coast is clear."

When the coast was clear? He had to snicker at that. All this cloak and dagger. It was starting to feel like he was suddenly dropped into an episode of Dragnet. He resisted the urge to say 'Roger that' and just said "Sounds good," and turned the corner.

◆◆◆

Ten minutes later he was parking in the very same spot in front of the gallery as he had before. He saw Darcy at the door waving him inside. He got out of the car and hustled over. "You have some information for me?" he asked.

"Yes, but let's get back to the office where we can't be seen," she said. She locked the door, then hurried back in that direction.

Isaac did the best he could to keep up.

He was told to sit in the same seat he had occupied during his interview with Dirk and Meredith. It was like déjà vu.

Darcy took the seat across the desk. "I um. I'm not sure where to begin." She said as she bit her lower lip nervously.

She seemed pretty distressed. Isaac used his best calming voice. "It's usually best to start at the beginning. How long have you been employed at *Perceptions*?"

"Only four months, but long enough to see what's going on here and I just need to get it off my chest."

"Oh? What's going on here?"

The corner of Darcy's mouth twitched. "I told her I wouldn't tell anyone, but with the death of Art, I just can't keep it secret any longer." She looked up to the ceiling then down into her lap. "Meredith is being blackmailed."

Isaac sat back in his seat. "Blackmailed?"

Darcy nodded. "Yes." She ran her hands through her short, dark hair. "She thought it was Art blackmailing her."

"I see. But let's back up a minute. How do you know she was being blackmailed? Did she tell you this?"

"I saw the letters." She bit her lip again. "I've been helping her with the drops."

"The drops?"

"The delivery of the money." She opened a file cabinet. "I have the letters," she said as she pulled out a large manilla envelope and handed it to Isaac. "Here they are."

Isaac carefully removed the letters from the envelope and placed them on the desk. Each one used cut out words and letters glued to the page. He knew they might be able to get some finger prints off of these, so once he'd read them, he slid them back in the envelope to preserve any evidence.

"Like I said, she thought it was Art." She shifted in her seat. "She hated him."

"Do you know why she was being blackmailed?"

The corner of her mouth twitched again. "She was having an affair."

Darcy was obviously wound up. She was like an entirely different person than the robot-like Darcy he encountered yesterday. "It's okay. I know you feel some loyalty to your friend," he said. "But you're doing the right thing by telling me all of this."

"She's a married woman and she was having an affair."

"And you don't approve."

"No, I don't approve, and I told her so." She crossed her arms across her chest.

"But you helped her with the money."

She bit her lip again. "Yes. I had to. I wanted to keep my job."

She was like a yo-yo coming unraveled then winding back up. But there was more to it than just her disapproval of the affair. He could feel it. Was it jealousy? he wondered. Isaac leaned in and folded his hands on the desk. In almost a whisper he said, "You don't like her much, do you?"

Darcy puffed out her chest, eyes on fire. "I just don't like that she was having an affair," she declared.

"I see," Isaac said.

She sat back and chewed on a cuticle. "I– I just don't like that she's having an affair," she repeated softly.

"Do you think Dirk knew about the affair?" Isaac asked.

"Oh no. Meredith took the money from the gallery account and marked it as an expense for Art so Dirk wouldn't know."

Isaac recalled Dirk saying he went to visit Art that fateful evening because of a large withdrawal from the gallery account. Could this withdrawal be one and the same? "Really. Do you recall the dates of these withdrawals?"

"Yes. June third and July first. They would be there in the books. Fifty thousand dollars each."

Isaac jotted that down. "Thank you." Now came the very important question he had been trying to answer since Cynthia's call. "Darcy, did Meredith suffer from depression?"

"What?" Darcy's eyes blinked rapidly. "Why would you ask that?"

"I'm just wondering about her state of mind," Isaac said. But what he really wanted to know was whether Meredith could be the source of the antidepressants that caused Artimus' paralysis. "What about Dirk, do you know if he suffered from depression?"

Darcy wrung her hands together. "How– how am I supposed to know that? What does that have anything to do with this?"

Isaac reached out his hands to her. "Okay, it's okay," he said calmly. "I wouldn't expect you to know that. It just seems that you do have quite a bit of important information, so I thought I'd ask."

"Well, Detective. Here's the most important information. I think she killed him. I think Meredith killed Art."

CHAPTER 24

Half an hour later, Isaac was back at the station. He wove his way through the paparazzi that were staking out the building and hounding all the officers who entered; their cacophony of questions all blurring together so that they just sounded like a flock of chickens. "No comment," he said to no one in particular.

"Isaac," Peg called when she saw him come through the door. "Come quick! I have news."

Isaac hustled over to her desk. "What's up?"

"They found Fiona Farkus on the security camera footage at the Rubber Bandits concert. She was there all night."

Isaac took the report from her hands.

"That's good news for Vick, right? They'll take him off leave now, right?"

Isaac put a hand on shoulder. "I don't know, Peg."

"But he's cleared. He was telling the truth. She *does* have an alibi."

"I'm sorry, Peg. That's for the board to decide."

She pouted. "It's all that Mimi Winslow's fault."

Isaac tapped the report. "Does Petruco know about this?"

"I don't think so because I don't see him out there entertaining the press. He told me to tell you to meet him in room 104." She looked over at the clock. "He'll be here in 10 minutes or so."

"Okay, thanks. I'll give him the good news." Isaac made his way down the hallway to the meeting room deep in thought. In addition to the confirmation that they could remove Fiona as a suspect, he had much to ponder and report after the interviews of the day. Something was pulling at him down deep in his gut. He couldn't put a finger on it yet, but it was there. The hunch he'd been waiting for. He knew he was on to something, but he didn't know just what.

He pulled open the door to the meeting room to find a familiar face leaning over the table, examining the photos spread all about. Isaac grinned wide. "Tom! You're back!" he said happily.

Tom looked up. "Hey Isaac. I am indeed. I was summoned by the one and only Captain Petruco."

"My, my, you must be important."

"I believe his words were, "Get back here right away, or go look for another job."

"Ha! Well, I'm sorry you had to cut your vacation short, but I'm sure glad you're back."

"Of course. I'd never leave you hanging, Jefe."

Isaac smiled hearing the nickname Tom had given him when Tom was taking his Spanish course. "So, getting yourself up to speed?"

"Yep. I was saddened to hear it was Artimus."

"You knew who Artimus was?"

"Yeah. Big fan. I have one of his prints."

"No kidding. We do too." Isaac scratched his head. "Although I didn't know it until Claudia pointed it out to me," he admitted.

"But I'm even more saddened to find out what a sleezy guy he was." Tom gestured at the photos and reports littering the table. "You wouldn't know it from his paintings."

"Right?"

Just then, Captain Petruco burst through the door. He looked back and forth at them. "Good." He pointed at Tom. "Welcome back."

"Thanks, Captain," Tom responded.

Petruco clapped his hands together. "Okay. Okay. Enough of the pleasantries, let's get on with it. Everybody sit."

Isaac and Tom took seats across from each other.

Petruco started to pace. "So, what new information do you have for me? I can't keep dodging the press like this. That Vick really screwed up. It's all I'm hearing about."

He looked stressed. After Mimi's interview with Fiona, and Vick's cameo appearance, the press were having a field day. The speculations and accusations were all over the board. But the main topic was the ineptitude of the police department. "I have some good news for you on that front, Captain," Isaac said. "We were able to locate Fiona Farkus at the Rubber Bandits concert on the security cameras, and she was there all night. Vick was correct. Fiona Farkus has a solid alibi."

Petruco clasped his hands together and looked to the sky. "Hallelujah!" he exclaimed. Then he raised his bushy brows and a scowl appeared on his face. "So when was someone going to tell me about it? Why am I the last to know?"

"I just found out about it myself, Captain," Isaac said.

He leaned on the table and looked Isaac right in the eyes. "I'm the Captain. Don't you think they should tell me first?"

"Of course they should," Isaac agreed. "That's why they entrusted me to make sure you were the first to know." Which really didn't make sense, but Isaac had learned over the years that a little bit of accolade was all it took to subdue Petruco.

"Well, yeah. Okay. Okay, then." He shoved his hands in his pockets and resumed pacing. "That's good news for the department, but now we're left with no suspects."

"I think I can help with that too," Isaac said. "I just had a couple of interesting interviews."

Petruco stopped in his tracks, his hands deep in his pockets, hunched over in his signature vulture pose staring intently at the floor. "Good. Tell me."

"My first interview of the day was with the owner of the gallery where Artimus shows his work – the same man Artimus was awarded the medal of honor for saving. Dirk Stanton. He admitted to being at Artimus' home that evening."

"Ah ha!" Petruco held his pointer finger to the sky. "If he was the last to see him alive, he must be our killer!"

Tom raised his hand. "I know I just arrived and am not totally up to speed, but did we determine that Artimus' death was a homicide?" He paged through the pages in front of him. "I didn't see that in the notes."

Isaac made a steeple of his fingers. As much as he wanted to, he couldn't reveal that Cynthia had confirmation that the death was not accidental. "Well no, but as standard procedure, we're investigating it as a homicide until we have the examiner's report to show otherwise."

Tom nodded. "Got it. Of course."

"And where *is* that examiner's report?" Petruco groused. "What can possibly be taking this long?" He looked at Isaac. "Who did you say was doing it?"

"Cynthia Chu, Captain." Isaac grinned mischievously at Tom. "I'm sure Tom would be happy to call Cynthia to find out for you sir."

Tom gave Isaac a dirty look.

"Good." Petruco pointed his finger at Tom. "Do that."

"Sure, Captain," Tom said. "But since Isaac is much more familiar with this case, don't you think it better that he contact her?"

Petruco looked back and forth between them, his forehead furrowed. "What the hell? I don't care who does it. Just do it." He returned to pacing. "Continue with your report, Isaac."

"Right. So not only does he admit to being there, but he says that Artimus was heavily intoxicated when he arrived." Isaac paused. "And he admits to striking Artimus."

"Well, let's get him back for more questioning!" Petruco shouted. "We can arrest him then."

"It gets a bit more complicated than that, Captain."

Petruco switched directions. "I'm listening."

"I then had an interview with the assistant to the gallery owner's wife. She says that *Mrs.* Stanton was being blackmailed for having an affair."

Petruco did an about face and started back the other way. "So?"

Isaac pulled out a manila envelope from his briefcase. "She gave me the actual blackmail letters. There are two." He laid them on the table.

Petruco stopped in front of the table to look at the letters.

Tom leaned across to do the same. "Wow. How did she have them?"

"She said she was helping drop the blackmail money. She said Mrs. Stanton believed the blackmailer was Artimus."

Petruco pulled a pen from his pocket and used it to move the top letter aside. "And?"

"And this assistant also believes Mrs. Stanton killed Artimus."

"Wait," Tom interjected. "To be clear, are we talking about *Meredith* Stanton?"

"Yes," Isaac responded.

Tom shuffled through and picked up a page off the table. "A report just came in from a neighbor who said they saw a red Corvette leaving Artimus' residence that evening." He looked up at them. "I also saw a report in here somewhere that Meredith Stanton drives a red Corvette."

"They're both in on it!" Petruco called out.

Isaac shook his head. "I don't know, Captain. Ms. Stanton seemed quite surprised to learn her husband had been at Artimus' that evening. I don't think they were in cahoots."

Petruco rubbed his chin. He'd worked with Isaac long enough to know that Isaac's instincts were spot on. "Well, I think we can agree that they are both suspects, is that correct?" He looked to Isaac for an answer.

Isaac thought for a moment. Did he? What exactly was this feeling he was having. How he wished he could put a finger on it. "Given this information, we'll at least want to question them again. I think it would be best if we questioned them separately."

"Good," Petruco said. He tucked the pen back in his pocket. "Let's bring the wife in first." He leaned down and tapped his pointer finger on the table. "And find out when we can expect to see the examiner's report." He straightened up and fixed his tie. "Now that we have the proof that Artimus' sister had an alibi, and that Mimi Winslow was wrong." He ran a hand over his head to smooth his slick-backed hair. "I'm going to go address the press." And with that he left the room.

"Jefe," Tom said once the door closed behind Petruco. "I thought you were my friend. How could you offer me up to call Cynthia?"

Isaac slapped Tom on the shoulder. "Just playing with you, Partner. I'll call her."

Tom cringed. "Believe it or not, she's already left me messages."

"I'm not surprised."

"How did she find out I was back so quickly?"

Isaac smiled. "She's been counting the days until your return," he said. "I was given specific instruction to let you know that you may have the honor of meeting with her this week so she can go through all the gory details of the autopsy – and you may even get a front row seat to watch her examine the cadaver."

Tom sat back in his seat, threw his pencil down on the table and put his hands to his head. "Eeaauuu," he groaned.

CHAPTER 25

"I'm here to get what's mine," Fiona declared as she entered the gallery.

Meredith's eyebrows raised. "Oh? Okay then. Please come on in." When Fiona called earlier and requested this meeting, Meredith expected that this was what it was about. Fiona obviously had no idea what their arrangement was with Art. Meredith stepped aside and let Fiona through the door, then locked it behind her. She extended her hand. "I'm Meredith, the curator."

"I'm Fiona, Artimus' sister," Fiona responded.

"Yes, I know. I'm so sorry about how Mimi treated you in that interview. She had no right to make such speculations."

Fiona nodded and pushed back the tears. It had been an emotional time. She figured her tears could have filled the pool Art drowned in. Was it true what Mimi had said about her family? How was she ever to know? There was no one she could check with – no one left in her family that could verify or debunk it. By telling her story to the world on nationwide television, Mimi had made it the truth. Whether it was or not, it's what people would now believe. She thought she finally had the flood waters under control and could move forward until just this moment. She squared her shoulders and cleared her throat. "Thanks," she said. "Mimi's a bitch."

Fiona's words were tough, but Meredith heard the crack in her voice. "Come on, let's go get an Arnie Palmer," she said. "It's sweltering out there." Meredith headed toward the kitchen area.

Fiona followed.

Meredith pulled the lemonade out of the refrigerator and placed it on the counter. She wasn't surprised Fiona was struggling to hold it all together. "You poor thing, Mimi really ambushed you," she said. She reached back into the refrigerator and pulled out the pitcher of iced tea. "It was cruel of her, and I want you to know that I was appalled by it."

Nice words, Fiona thought to herself. But were they genuine? She knew nothing about this woman, so she wasn't going to let her guard down. People could hurt you. Even people you thought were trustworthy. "Thanks," Fiona said. "It *was* cruel." She scowled. "I don't like it when people take advantage of me."

Meredith's heart went out to her. It was evident that interview had taken a toll on this young girl, and understandingly so. It was time to lighten the mood, she decided. "Believe me, we were very happy when the police verified your alibi proving Mimi wrong." Meredith smirked. "It was fun to see Mimi back-peddling."

Fiona couldn't help but smile at that.

"I hope she back peddles all the way to North Dakota!" Meredith added with a snort.

This was not going the way she had expected, Fiona thought to herself. Try as she might *not* to, she liked Meredith. Meredith seemed so *sincere*. Not like so many of the others who had been hounding her trying to lease space to her at exorbitant rates. She got the feeling those people just wanted to be a part of the gossip. Like they were enjoying all the drama. "I hope she back peddles all the way to the moon!" Fiona exclaimed.

Meredith let out a hoot and they shared a good laugh together. The ice had been broken.

Fiona took a deep breath. "This is not going at all the way I expected," she admitted out loud.

Meredith smiled knowing that was a good thing. "Please sit down." She handed Fiona her Arnie Palmer. "Let's talk."

Fiona took a seat across the table.

"So, first, tell me about what you're wearing," Meredith said, remembering how Fiona was trying to introduce her wearable art before she was so completely blindsided with accusations of having a murderous father and murdering her own brother.

Fiona lit up. "Sure!" She stood up and twirled. She took some time to tell Meredith about her process and the products she used to create her fashions. It was obvious she had longed to talk about it with someone who would actually listen.

Once Fiona had finished, Meredith said, "I can tell you put a lot of thought and effort into your creations."

"I do. They're all made to order originals," she said. "Not just copies of things like a well-known artist I know." There. It was out there. She sat back and waited to see if Meredith took the bait.

Meredith took a sip of her Arnie Palmer. So it was evident that they both knew the truth about Art's paintings, she thought to herself. She had been so grateful she stumbled upon his secret before anyone else did, but she should have guessed that a sister would know. Meredith would never forget stepping into Artimus' room and seeing that old overhead projector, the kind used in schools many years ago, pointing at a canvas hanging on the wall across the room. The canvas had some swipes of blue paint. Drape cloths covered the floor underneath it. Floor tiles were scattered about on the counter of the bar. All sorts of floor tiles – different types of marble, travertine, and onyx.

She had walked over to the projector and switched it on. An image projected onto the canvas. It looked like the color by number paintings one did as a kid. He wasn't a painter, she had realized. He copied his designs off pictures of floor tiles that had been printed on transparencies. All these years, he'd been passing himself off as some great artist while laughing all the way to the bank. She cringed inwardly. Since Art's passing, it had become her turn to keep his secret. Would sis go along? "Oh?" Meredith said.

Fiona smiled. She could see it in Meredith's eyes. Meredith knew. "Yes," Fiona said. "But I guess I'm the one to blame since I taught him how to do it."

♦♦♦

It had been just after her mother's death when life got so hard and Fiona desperately needed something to brighten her day. It all began with the transparency of the rose she "borrowed" from school. She hadn't *planned* to take it, but it was just so pretty - and she needed something pretty in her life just then. So, when the teacher wasn't looking, she slipped it into her backpack. She took it home, taped it to her window, and noticed that when the sun shined through, the rose appeared on the wall across the room. So, one day, she decided to paint it. The next day she moved the transparency and painted another, and the next day another, and another until the whole wall was filled with roses. Art would sometimes stop in to tell her to get off her ass and go do something like sweep the floor or make dinner or one of the many other chores she had inherited since the loss of her mother, and would watch her do it. It was the one and only time he would give her space. She thought it somehow brought some little bit of peace to both of them.

◆◆◆

She looked over at Meredith. "You needn't worry, though, they're much more valuable to me if no one knows."

Meredith nodded. But how will she feel once she finds out the paintings aren't hers, she wondered. "Let me tell you a story about those paintings," Meredith began. "When this gallery opened, they were selling for just fifty dollars apiece to the passersby of the gallery. And it would have continued on that way," she said, "simply because without a marketing plan they weren't attracting the right audience. But then I stepped in, remodeled the space, and changed the price to five thousand dollars apiece." She grinned like the Cheshire cat. "Your brother was unhappy with me at first. He had been selling four paintings a month, but with the price increase, was then only selling one. However," she held up her right index finger. "It didn't take long for him to realize that selling one painting for five thousand dollars was much better than getting less than a tenth of that amount for four." She held up her palms. "That sometimes selling less is more. With my head for marketing, we started getting noticed. First in the local community, then across the nation. And we continued to raise the price as the demand would allow. Eventually "Artimus" became a household word in the art world like Shakira and Usher are to music, and D-Wade and LeBron are to basketball."

Fiona beamed. Thanks to Meredith, her brother's copycat paintings were selling for big money. "So, how many paintings do you have?"

Meredith folded her hands in her lap. Here comes the difficult part, she thought to herself. "We have…. several," she said, leaving off the word 'hundred' from the end of her sentence.

"Okay," Fiona said happily, calculating the value in her head. "So how do I transport them? Is my car big enough?"

"Well, I'm afraid you won't have to worry about that."

"Oh? You'll deliver?"

"Well, no." Meredith looked into Fiona's eyes. "The paintings belong to the gallery."

"What?"

"Art was under contract with the gallery."

Fiona narrowed her eyes. "What kind of contact?"

"It was pretty straight forward, actually. The gallery would market his paintings, give him a place to paint, sell and store his works, and Art would get a percentage of the profits when a painting sold."

"Are you shittin' me? All that talk about how you took my brother's paintings and made them famous? Was that just to rub salt in the wound?"

Meredith shook her head. "No, no Fiona…." she began, but was interrupted by a knock at the door. Meredith stood and looked around the divider. "It's the police," she declared. "Whatever do they want now?" She took a deep breath. "I'd better see what this is about." She looked at Fiona. "You just stay there, I'll explain everything when I get back." Meredith headed toward the door.

Fiona stood and started after her. "If you think I'm just going to sit here and wait for you to twist the knife you've got another thing coming."

"Really Fiona, please, please just wait," Meredith said as she opened the door.

"Meredith Stanton?" the police officer asked.

"Yes," Meredith said. "What can I do for you officer?"

Fiona pushed past them through the door. "You're just like the rest of them," she said to Meredith. Then she turned toward the officer. "Yeah, arrest her officer. She's a cheat and a liar – and I can prove it."

CHAPTER 26

Isaac and Tom pushed open the door to the room where the officer had taken Meredith.

"Good afternoon," Isaac said to her.

"Detective!" Meredith exclaimed. "What's going on here? Why was I picked up in a squad car? Am I being arrested?"

Isaac took a seat across from her and laid the file on the table in front of him. This first sentence was always the worst. It needed to be said in a way that calmed the suspect down but didn't make any promises. Whether one is innocent or guilty, being brought into a police station for questioning is a harrowing experience. "Ms. Stanton," he began, "we brought you here so that we can talk with you without any interruptions or outside distractions." He gave her a kind smile. "We just want to get a little more information about Mr. Farkus and some other matters that have to do with this case and are hoping you can provide it for us."

"Information? What kind of information? I already told you everything I know, Detective."

Actually, he thought to himself, she had done just the opposite. She had given Isaac the sugar-coated version of the man known as Artimus. The one she projects to the art world to sell his works. Just what else was she covering up, he wondered. "Ms. Stanton, this is Detective Bryant. He'll be sitting in with us so we can get him up to speed on the case."

Tom stood and extended his hand across the table. "Nice to meet you," he said.

She apprehensively placed her fingers in his hand, then pulled them back. "I don't mean to be impertinent, but I'm not so sure it's nice to meet you, Detective."

"I understand your uneasiness, Ms. Stanton. But we'd appreciate just a few minutes of your time."

"Okay, I guess. I mean what choice do I have here?" She smoothed the fabric of her skirt. "So let's get on with it. I need to get back to the gallery."

"Thank you."

She flipped her long ponytail to her back. "What do you want to know?"

Isaac pulled a notepad from the file and placed it in front of him. He took a pen from his pocket and clicked it a few times. "Did Mr. Farkus have any enemies?" he asked.

"Detective, would you please stop calling him Mr. Farkus?" Meredith said. "Nobody knew him by that name. Just call him Art." Then added as an aside, "And you can call me Meredith."

Isaac rested his forearms on the table and crossed his fingers together. "Okay. Thank you," he acknowledged. "Meredith, did Art have any enemies?"

Since Dirk had already let the cat out of the bag, she wasn't going to try to shove it back in. "Probably tons. As Dirk told you, he wasn't a nice person."

"Do any particular people come to mind?"

She took in a deep breath and let it out slowly through her lips. "Enemies? No." She scratched her nose. "I'm just saying, if you were unfortunate enough to know Art, you didn't like him. Okay?"

"So you didn't like him?"

"No," she admitted. "I didn't like him."

"Can you give me specific reasons as to why you didn't like Art?" Isaac asked. He really didn't expect her to blurt out 'because he's blackmailing me,' but he'd had more surprising things happen in the past.

She shrugged. "Because he treated women like meat, he liked to degrade others, he took advantage of people, he was crude…" She shook her head. "I could go on, but I don't see the point. I think you get it."

"Okay. Yes. But is there anything else? Anything *specific* you can relate?"

Why did he keep asking her this? Did they find the damning photos at Art's house? But even if they did find them, how would they know anything was amiss? They wouldn't. They couldn't. Only she and Dirk would know. Still, she needed to put a stop to this. She placed her palms firmly on the table and looked Isaac in the eye. "Why do you keep asking me this, Detective? Do you think I killed him? Because I will tell you right now. I didn't."

Tom began to pull out the folder with the blackmail letters, but Isaac put a hand on them. Isaac had heard many a guilty person declare their innocence before and found that it was a cue to change the line of questioning. Pushing further would do more harm than good. Changing the subject will throw the suspect off. Moreover, he could then get to what he really wanted to know. Isaac tapped his pen on the table. "Do you know if Art suffered from anxiety or depression?" he asked.

Tom sat back, a bit flummoxed by Isaac's change in direction. It had seemed to Tom like Isaac was right on track to reveal the blackmail letters, but Tom also knew from past experience that if Isaac Scott felt this was the best course to take, he shouldn't question it.

Meredith furrowed her brow and sat back in her seat with a sigh of relief. "I honestly don't know. But I wouldn't be surprised if he did. He was in the service. Many veterans do." She raised her brows. "But if you're wondering if he was suicidal, Detective, I'd say absolutely not. He loved himself too much to do that."

"Do you know if he was taking any medications?"

She let out a snort. "No, I don't." She rubbed her forehead. "You know, Detective, if you brought me here thinking I was close to Art because we worked together, you are sorely mistaken. Even though he saved my husband's life, we tried to have as little of a relationship with Art as possible. I know very little about his personal life." She threw up her hands. "I mean, I didn't even know he had a sister!"

"That's right," Isaac said as if just remembering. "Your husband was in the service with Art. Does your husband take any medications for anxiety or depression?"

"Detective," Meredith began. "My husband was severely injured." More by the bullets that hit him in the back while being carried by Art as a shield, than the explosion that initially knocked him out, she didn't add. "He was hospitalized for three months and is still going through PT. He takes <u>lots</u> of pills for all kinds of different things." She looked directly at Isaac. "If you are insinuating that my husband had anything to do with the death of Art, you are very mistaken. There isn't a better, kinder, more patient soul on this earth."

Those certainly didn't sound like the words of a woman who was having an affair, Isaac thought to himself. "Well, I'm glad to hear that you have such a happy marriage. Not many couples can say that."

"We do. I would do anything for my husband."

Anything? Would she kill for her husband? It certainly sounded like she had access to the kind of drug that Artimus had in his system. "Ms. Stanton, you said you were out with friends on the night Art died. Is that correct?"

She crossed one leg over the other. "Yes. Out with friends."

"Good. Could you tell us their names and give us their contact information so we can call and confirm? You know, just to have your alibi of record."

She looked down into her lap. "Detective, why do I need an alibi?"

"Ms. Stanton, it's our job to eliminate and document those with alibis so we have a clearer path to follow if it turns out that Art was murdered. So, once we have the names of your friends, and your alibi is confirmed, we can put that in the file and move forward."

She cringed. "Well actually, it was just one friend," she admitted.

"Okay. That's fine. One friend. And what's the friend's name?"

She closed her eyes and let out a sigh. "I can't tell you that."

"And why is that?"

"We have an agreement."

"An agreement?" Isaac turned and nodded at Tom. He held out his hand to take the folder Tom had offered him earlier.

Tom pulled it out and gave it to him.

Isaac opened the folder and withdrew one of the ransom notes that had been covered in plastic and placed it on the table in front of her. "Ms. Stanton, what can you tell us about this?"

She gasped. "Where did you get that?" Why hadn't Darcy shredded this? she thought with alarm.

"That's not important," Isaac said. "To what *pictures* is this note referring?"

She put her head in her hands. "I know what you're thinking, but I'm not having an affair."

"Ms. Stanton," Tom chimed in. "A red Corvette was seen leaving Art's residence that evening. Yet you say you weren't there?"

"Detective, I'm not the only one who drives a red corvette." She was getting bombarded. She looked back and forth between them. "Don't I get a phone call or something?"

Given the evidence, it was certainly understandable she would want an attorney present, Isaac thought to himself. But was it just because of the blackmail? Because of the murder? Or because of both? He wished he could get his head around all the mixed messages that were coming in. She seemed so sincere and innocent, yet the evidence was building against her. He just couldn't decipher it. She was a dichotomy. Like the color orange. "Of course," he responded.

♦♦♦

Isaac and Tom got the call to return half an hour later. They rounded the corner to head down the hall to the meeting room, when Isaac stopped in his tracks. He saw the sandy haired gentlemen heading toward them. Meredith had called her husband? Creases appeared on his forehead. That didn't make any sense – especially given the blackmail information they had.

Tom turned towards Isaac. "What's up, Jefe?" he asked, then followed Isaac's eyes to see what had caught his attention. A smile came to Tom's face. "Hey!" Tom called out to the man.

Isaac leaned over and whispered in Tom's ear. "That's Meredith's husband."

Tom gave Isaac a bewildered glance, then high-tailed it over to greet the man.

Isaac watched as they shared a hearty handshake.

"What brings you here?" Tom asked him.

"I'm visiting my folks. They're over at Friendship Village. I come once a month to check in on them," the man replied. He slapped Tom on the arm. "I heard you were here in Minneapolis, dude." Then a look of concern came over his face. "How're you doing, man?" he asked remembering the tragic loss of Tom's fiancé just about a year ago.

"Hanging in there." Tom said. "This was a good change for me."

Isaac came to Tom's side with a look of confusion on his face.

Tom put a hand on his shoulder. "Isaac," Tom said. "I'd like you to meet Gabe Parrington. An old friend and colleague of mine from Wisconsin."

"Nice to meet you, Gabe," Isaac said as he reached out his hand. "I apologize for staring," he said. "It's just that you look exactly like –"

"Dirk Stanton?" Gabe said finishing his sentence. He smiled. "Yes, I know. That's why I'm here. Meredith called me."

Isaac raised his eyebrows. "She did?" He gestured toward the door. "Okay then. Let's go into the meeting room, shall we?"

"Gabe!" Meredith called as he entered the room. She got up and gave him a friendly handshake, grasping his hand with both of hers. "Thank you so much for coming."

"Of course," he responded. He took a seat next to her. "Meredith called me because I am her alibi for the night of Artimus' death. We've been meeting monthly - when I'm here to see my parents. She was with me the night Artimus drown." He looked over at Meredith and gave her a nod. "I'll let Meredith explain."

"Yes. Well, I'm not sure where to start, but the first thing I want you both to know is that this thing between us," she pointed back and forth between herself and Gabe with her pointer finger. "Is not an affair."

"That's right," Gabe confirmed.

"You see," she continued. "Dirk, my husband, and I always wanted to have a family. It was something we both dreamed of. But the injuries he suffered in Afghanistan left him unable to…" she paused looking for the right word. "Produce children." She looked to the ceiling. "So, we did a lot of research, and after some consideration, we decided to consult with a fertility clinic." She pulled her ponytail back over her shoulder. "So anyway, during the time we were searching for solutions to our problem, I came across a method," she paused and looked back and forth between them, "FDA approved, mind you," she added, feeling the need to clarify that it wasn't something unsafe or unfounded. "For at-home insemination by self-injecting sperm," she said. "But at the time it really didn't apply to me." She clasped her hands together and brought them to her chest. "But then one day, out of the blue, I bumped into Gabriel at the Mall of America."

"Actually, I bumped into her," he corrected with a smile.

"Yes, that's right." She laughed. "Well, you can imagine, Detective, when I saw him, I just couldn't believe my eyes. He was the spitting image of Dirk. It was just remarkable, and I found myself following him through the Mall."

It was Gabe's turn to chuckle. "So, when I was in line at the food court, I felt a little tap on my shoulder, and turned to find Meredith behind me. She told me that I looked exactly like her husband, and she showed me some photos." He held his palms to the sky. "It was true. He looked just like me."

"I asked if I might have a minute of his time," Meredith said. "And offered to take him to dinner."

"And, maybe it's the police officer in me, but there was just something in her eyes that made me feel I should. So, I accepted her invitation. Over dinner, she told me their story and asked if I would be willing to help them. I took the next couple of months to think it over," he told them. "It wasn't an easy decision, but I kept thinking about all Dirk went through for all of us by serving our County and I decided to go forward with the provisos that first, either one of us could end this at any time, and second, that it be held strictly confidential between the three of us." He gestured toward Meredith. "I am very grateful for the service of men like Dirk. Their sacrifices keep our country safe. I decided it was a way to help a fellow officer."

"So, I had my attorney draw up the papers." She looked across the table at Isaac and Tom. "And that's how it began."

"In a nutshell," Gabe said.

"I want to be sure you understand, Detectives, there was never any physical relationship between us. This was a business arrangement, not an affair."

"That's correct," Gabe confirmed.

She looked gratefully over at him. "I just knew that Gabe's DNA would give us the best chance of having a child that looked like it was conceived by my husband and me."

"And after my dealings with Meredith, I knew that child would be raised in a home filled with love."

There was a moment of silence.

"So you were there together all night that night?" Isaac asked.

"Well not together," Gabe said. "But…"

"You see, Detective," Meredith interjected. "The fresher the sperm, the better the chance it has to reach and fertilize the egg." She blushed. "And the woman needs to stay in a prone position for a few hours after the injection, so I just stayed in Gabe's hotel room."

"That's right," Gabe confirmed. "I gave Meredith my um, *contribution*, then went to the bar downstairs and watched the Twins' game. Meredith waved to me on her way out. It was about nine o'clock by then. So, I can attest that Meredith was in my hotel room from just after six o'clock until nine o'clock that evening."

"How can you be sure she didn't leave out a different exit?" Isaac asked.

"I could see her car from the bar. I didn't ever notice it missing."

"And you were monitoring it the whole time? Even while watching the game?" Tom asked.

"Not closely," Gabe said. "But I believe I would have noticed if it were gone. You see, if it were gone, it would mean I could go back to my hotel room."

"Oh, I was there," Meredith said. "I watched a movie. It was a Sherlock Holmes movie. The second one. *A Game of Shadows*," she told them. "Which is exactly what *this* feels like," she said. She looked across the table at Isaac. "Detective, where did you get those blackmail letters?"

"I'm sorry, I can't disclose that information," Isaac told her.

"Blackmail letters?" Gabe asked.

"Detective, did Darcy give them to you?" Meredith raised her brows. "Because Darcy was the one driving my red Corvette that evening."

Gabe frowned. "Darcy? Who's Darcy?"

Meredith looked over at Gabe and let out a deep sigh. "She's my assistant." She let her head drop. "And I thought she was my friend," she added. "When all the while she could have been setting me up." She put her hand to her forehead. "Someone has pictures of us together at dinner at the Mall of America and has been blackmailing me." She took a deep breath. "I didn't tell you about this, because, well, I didn't want you to know that I hadn't told Dirk about our arrangement yet."

"You didn't tell your husband about this?" Gabe exclaimed as he jumped out of his seat.

She looked down in her lap and shook her head. "I was going to ..." she began.

"You were going to?" Gabe gasped. "Meredith, that was a big part of our agreement." He put a hand to his head. "I thought he knew. Shame on you."

"I know, I know. I just couldn't figure out how to broach the subject with him." She covered her face with her hands. "And I was just so worried he would say no, and I didn't want him to. I so wanted this to work." She looked up at Gabe with sad, apologetic eyes. "And I believe it will work. I'm so sorry, Gabe."

Gabe rubbed the back of his neck and let out a groan, his head spinning.

Meredith turned her attention to Isaac and Tom. "Given what you've got here, I'm wondering if Darcy and Art were somehow working together on this blackmailing. Could it be that something went wrong between them that evening? Something so wrong that Art ended up dead?"

CHAPTER 27

Tom and Isaac escorted Meredith and Gabe out of the station and into a squad car through a back entrance to avoid the press.

"Do you think we can officially check Meredith off the suspect list?" Isaac asked Tom.

"Yeah," Tom said. "Gabe's a good man. I take him at his word. We served together in Madison, you know. What a coincidence, huh Jefe?"

Isaac shook his head in wonder. "I'm telling you," he said. "I've never seen two people, other than twins, that look as much alike as those two. Even the way they wear their hair. It's uncanny."

"Yeah, that's so weird," Tom said. "I look forward to meeting Mr. Stanton to see for myself." He put a hand to his chin. "You know, even though Meredith is pointing a finger at Darcy, I don't think we can rule Mr. Stanton out. You tell me he admits to being there and striking Artimus."

"Agreed. Certainly Meredith would be inclined to divert our attention away from him."

"Should I have him picked up?"

Isaac pinched the bridge of his nose. "Petruco will want us to interview him next." Things at the station had calmed down a bit since the Mimi Winslow interview and Vick's cameo appearance. The department had fortunately been vindicated by being able to confirm that Fiona had an alibi, but they were dealing with an international media, so there was no lapse of news coverage and the reporters were relentless. Even Petruco was getting tired of seeing his face on television. "But, I think we should speak with Darcy first," Isaac said. "She was quite agitated when she gave me the blackmail letters."

"Agitated? That could go either way, don't you think?" Tom held out his right hand. "Was Darcy agitated because she really thought Meredith killed Artimus, or," he held out his left hand. "Was she setting Meredith up?"

"Exactly what we need to find out," Isaac said.

"Then should I have Darcy picked up?"

Isaac shook his head. "Unfortunately, it's all going to have to wait until tomorrow. I need to get Avery to her counseling appointment this afternoon."

"Aw, sweet Avery," Tom said with a smile. "How's it going for her?"

"Good, I think. This will be her last appointment," Isaac told him. "Believe it or not, she says she prefers talking with me, because I can understand."

"So true, Jefe." Tom slapped him on the back. "You're an amazing dad and a great officer. Makes total sense to me."

✦✦✦

Isaac came home to find his three children running through the sprinkler in his front yard. He stopped in the driveway and laughed out loud as Avery leaped over with a high-pitched screech.

Edna lifted up the wide brim of her bright yellow sun hat and waved to him from her lawn chair that was tucked under the shade of the old maple tree. "You-hoo, Detective!" she called.

Isaac rolled down his window. "Hey Edna!" he called back.

Jacob jumped over the top of the sprinkler like a wide receiver going in for a touchdown, and Isabelle followed with a pirouette.

"Hey Avery!" Isaac hollered. He motioned for her to come to his side.

Avery looked over at him, hung her head low, then slogged through the soggy grass and stood by the car dripping wet. "Hi dad," she mumbled when she reached his side.

"Go on in now and get dried off and dressed. We've got to go to your appointment," he told her.

"Aww, dad." She pouted. "But we're having so much fun. Do we have to?"

"Yes, dear. We have to. Now go inside, dry off, and get dressed."

She glanced back over her shoulder at the other kids. "But, dad…"

"You can run through the sprinkler another time, young lady."

She frowned at him for a long moment, then turned and skulked over to the front stoop, grabbed a towel and disappeared through the front door.

Isaac heard Jacob call out to him "Hey Detective, watch this!" Then he stuck his face right over the sprinkler head and water shot out in all directions.

Isabelle laughed and ran around swishing her hands through the spray.

Isaac smiled. There was nothing like a sprinkler on a hot, July day. He rolled up his window and pulled into the garage.

Walter greeted him with a lunge at his midsection, but Isaac was too quick and jumped aside. Walter turned and came towards him again, tag wagging, taking his whole rear end back and forth along with it.

Isaac leaned down and pet his head. "Hey Walter. I'm glad to see you too, dog."

Isaac walked around to the stairway with Walter at his heels. He called up to Avery. "Hurry up, kiddo. We have to leave in fifteen minutes!"

He turned and took a seat on a step and let his head drop. He stared down at the travertine tile that covered their entry floor. Each piece unique. Just like the tiles found in the dumpster. Why were there so many in there, he wondered. And so many different kinds? He let his eyes wander across the floor toward the living room then up to the print of the Artimus painting hanging over their couch. A crease appeared on his forehead. He looked back at the tile, then up to the painting again. A light went on inside his head. He stood and walked over to the painting. His eyes wandered around it taking in the sweeps of color. Was it that simple?

"Ha!" he exclaimed with delight. "Are you a painting of a floor tile?" he wondered aloud. He rubbed his chin as it all came together. The dents in the basement carpet were about the size of the old overhead projector found in the dumpster, and the strips of plastic could be shredded transparencies. Yes, yes, he thought to himself. It all made sense. "Ha!" he exclaimed again. Was that what Meredith had been so worried he'd find when they searched the dumpster? Because it was certain that if word got out that Artimus was just copying the designs on floor tiles, the value of his paintings would drop like a rock. Every DIYer would just be doing it for themselves, and others would be ordering "Artimus-like" paintings from other crafty people on Etsy. Still, Isaac thought as he stared a bit longer at the painting, he needed to give Artimus his due. Not everyone could do it like this. This one was nicely done.

He continued to let his eyes follow the swirls of color hoping for some vibe, some inspiration, to help him solve the mystery of what happened the night Artimus drowned. Since they hadn't been able to find any pill bottles anywhere in Artimus' home, studio or car, it had become clear to Isaac that someone else aided in Artimus' death. But who? Why? Not his sister, Fiona, and not Meredith. Could it be Darcy as Meredith suspected? Could it be Dirk? Could all the years of resentment between them overflowed that night? Dirk said Art was drunk when he arrived, but according to what Cynthia discovered, it was also something else. A TCA. Perhaps Art wasn't goading Dirk at all, but was just so incapacitated he was unable to respond.

He felt a tap on his shoulder. "I'm ready," Avery said.

He turned to find her dressed, with a head full of dripping wet curls. "Do you want to take a minute to dry your hair?"

She shrugged. "Nah, it'll help keep me cooler this way."

He shrugged. "Okay."

And off they went.

"Are you sure you're ready to be done with the counseling, Avery?" Isaac asked.

"Yeah, Dad. I'm okay. I've had enough counseling," she said, then turned and looked at him with searching eyes. "But I'd still like to talk with you, okay?"

"Of course, sweetheart. You know I'm always here for you." He reached out and took her hand and gave it a squeeze.

"Thanks, Dad."

Once they arrived, Avery checked in and was taken to the counselor's office. Isaac had already spoken with the counselor about this being Avery's last session, and the counselor agreed that Avery was ready. Isaac settled into a chair in the corner of the crowded waiting room and pulled out the Star Tribune newspaper he'd brought with him to read while he waited.

Patients came and went, and the clock ticked on.

About 10 minutes before Avery was to be done with her session, Isaac heard an angry voice coming from the check-in desk.

All the heads in the waiting room popped up in curiosity.

With each exchange, the volume increased and the atmosphere in the waiting room became more disturbed.

People's eyes darted about the room. Worry and confusion appeared on their faces. Being that incomprehensible acts of violence had been happening across the U.S., and they happened to be in a waiting room for people dealing with psychiatric issues, their concern was rightfully heightened. One woman stood and ushered her teenager out of the office. Another man took a seat closer to the door. Isaac patted his jacket to check on his firearm.

At first it was hard to hear what the issue was, but when she'd reached her boiling point, the woman banged her fist on the plexiglass separator causing several patrons to jump up out of their seats and rush toward the door. "I need my Pronorfranil!" she yelled.

Isaac couldn't make out the response from the receptionist, but it was obvious that it wasn't what the woman wanted to hear.

She stamped her foot. "I know it's a regulated substance!" she howled. "Like I told you, I dropped my purse, and the bottle with the pills fell into the sewer drain! How many times do I have to explain this? Are you deaf?"

The rattled receptionist must have asked the woman to follow her to a room, because the last thing Isaac heard was.

"Why do I have to wait in a room? I just need my prescription re-filled!"

He watched as the receptionist stood and started down the hallway.

The incensed woman snarled, then bent down to snatch her purse from the floor and that's when he saw her face. He knew that face.

CHAPTER 28

Isaac stepped out into the hallway of the counselor's building, pulled his cell phone from his pocket and dialed. "This is Isaac Scott, may I speak to Dr. Chu, please?"

"Just a moment," came the answer from the other end of the line.

He heard Cynthia come on the line and holler out "Close that door tightly this time, you simpleton!"

She sounded particularly ferocious, Isaac thought to himself. But he knew that wasn't directed at him.

"Isaac?" she said. "I didn't expect to hear from *you*. I've been leaving messages for Detective Bryant. Isn't he back in town?"

Isaac didn't want to go there. He decided to get right to the point and bypassed her question. "Cynthia, is Pronorfranil one of the TCAs that was found in Artimus' body?"

"It could be. I still don't have the reports back from those imbeciles in toxicology, but that would give the type of results we have."

Interesting. "If given a large amount of Pronorfranil, what types of symptoms would someone on this medication have?"

"Well Isaac, you know as well as I do that it's impossible to give a concise answer to such an open-ended question. It would depend on the dose. I would need more information. What do you mean by a "large amount"? I mean, symptoms can range from headache, dry mouth, and fever, to life threatening symptoms like confusion, hallucinations, seizure, rapid heart rate, tremors, coma, and cardiac arrest to name a few. An overdose of a TCA causes Serotonin Syndrome."

"Serotonin Syndrome?"

"Yes. It's what causes those symptoms I mentioned. It happens when too much serotonin builds up in the body."

"What if the TCA is mixed with alcohol?"

"Again, Isaac," she said condescendingly. "It would depend on the amount, but in every case, those symptoms would be exacerbated."

"Thank you," Isaac said. "Can you give me an idea when we can expect the examiner's report to be ready?" he asked.

"It will be ready when it's ready," she answered tersely. "It seems I have a leak in this department," she snarled, referring to how Mimi Winslow obtained a copy of the preliminary results. "And it would in your best interests to find out just who that is. Perhaps that would speed up the process around here. Right now, I don't trust ANYONE. Do you understand? I'm handling this. I will review the test results myself as they come in. Artimus deserves that. Now if you want it to move along more quickly, I would suggest you get Detective Bryant over here to help me."

"I think Captain Petruco has him tied up with other matters right now, Cynthia. But I will send your message."

"You can tell Captain Petruco that he better get his priorities straight because if he doesn't plug the leak in my office, he'll have to deal with more incidents like the one with that Winslow woman." And with that, she hung up.

Isaac dialed the number for Tom and listened to it ring.

"Hey Jefe," Tom answered.

"Sorry to call you so late," Isaac said. "But I've got some news for you."

"And I've got some news for you, too," Tom replied. "Turns out, Gabe had a few dates with a girl named Darcy. He cut it off pretty quickly though, but she wouldn't let go and continued to call him to the point that he had to change his number. From what he said, it sounds like *that* Darcy had some trouble telling the truth."

"That certainly is interesting – especially given what I have just learned. Can you meet me at the station in a half hour?"

"I'm already there. I'll see you when you get here."

♦♦♦

Having obtained a search warrant, uniformed officers showed up at Darcy's apartment at eight o'clock the next morning and ushered her to the squad car while the forensics team moved into her apartment.

Darcy was fingerprinted and escorted to the interrogation room.

The lab had been able to get some partial fingerprints off the blackmail letters – and most importantly from the backs of the pieces of paper used for the lettering. They had not, however, been able to find a match in their system. Isaac was feeling quite confident that those fingerprints would match Darcy's.

Tom and Isaac ushered Gabe into the room on the other side of the two-way mirror from where Darcy had been seated.

Petruco stopped his pacing and looked up at them as they entered.

"Is that her?" Tom asked Gabe.

Gabe looked through the window and let his head drop. "Yes, that's her."

"Okay. Thanks for bringing this to our attention, dude," Tom said.

"That's a big piece to the puzzle," Isaac added.

"I'm just stunned," Gabe said. He had contacted Tom after their meeting with Meredith yesterday. Darcy was not the most common name, and he thought it best to inform Tom about his recent history with a certain Darcy in Wisconsin – just to be sure Meredith's Darcy wasn't that same person. But it was. "I'm glad Meredith mentioned her name."

"Captain," Tom said. "This is Gabe Parrington. Gabe and I worked together in Wisconsin."

Gabe held out his hand to Petruco.

Petruco stared at him. "So, that's your old girlfriend, huh?" he said. "So, you're the reason for all this trouble?"

Gabe blinked. "What?" He pulled his hand back.

Petruco pointed a finger at Darcy sitting in the other room. "You brought that murderous Wisconsin cheesehead into our fair city."

Gabe stood straighter. "Forgive me, Captain, but I most certainly did not."

"Do you think she'd be here if it wasn't for you?"

"I have no idea – but –" he sputtered.

"Captain, Gabe's here to help," Tom interjected.

"I had nothing to do with her coming here," Gabe declared. "I have no control over her. She came of her own free will."

Petruco put his hands on his hips and leaned forward. "Sure, of her own free will." He narrowed his hawk eyes at Gabe. "Because of you."

Isaac stepped up between them. "Captain, I'm sure Gabe is as eager to get to the bottom of this as we are."

"That's right," Gabe said. "But – "

Tom put a hand on Gabe's shoulder. "But he needs to get back to his elderly parents just now," he said, trying to avoid further provocation.

"Do you have any idea how much trouble this vixen has caused us?" Petruco asked. "She's probably responsible for the death of the largest luminary in this state. Known worldwide. My phone hasn't stopped ringing. The press won't leave me alone. So okay," Petruco said, his beady eyes on Gabe. "You want my forgiveness? I'll forgive you." He pushed his pointer finger into Gabe's chest. "If you help us nail her."

Gabe took a step back and curbed his desire to say no more than, "Of course I will, Captain."

Isaac and Tom let out a collective sigh of relief.

"We better get over there," Isaac said to Tom. He turned toward Petruco. "Captain, if you have any comments or questions, Peg can deliver them to us."

"Good," Petruco said. "Let's get this done."

Isaac, Tom, and Gabe headed for the door.

"Whoa, Wisconsin boy," Petruco said to Gabe. "You're not going anywhere. Take a seat. I want you to see this whole thing. You're here to help us, remember?"

Gabe sighed and pinched the bridge of his nose. "Yeah," he said. He pulled out the stool closest to the door, but before taking a seat he put a hand on Tom's arm. "Remember," he warned him. "She's a liar. And she's good at it."

◆ ◆ ◆

In minutes Gabe and Petruco watched Isaac and Tom enter the room across from them.

"Good morning," Isaac said. He set the file down as he and Tom took seats across from Darcy.

"What's so good about it? Doesn't seem so good on this side of the table," Darcy said. "Why did you bring me here like this, Detective? Am I being charged with something? Because I haven't heard anyone read me my rights yet."

"No charges have been brought against you," Isaac confirmed. At least not yet, he didn't add. "Would you like your attorney present?"

"I don't have an attorney," she grunted.

"Public defender, then?"

She crossed her arms over her chest. "I don't need one."

"Okay, then. Let's get going, shall we? We'd like to ask you some more questions about the blackmail letters and Artimus."

"You guys must be really struggling with this. Kind of grasping at straws? Otherwise, I don't know why you'd bring me in here. I have nothing more to tell you."

Over the years, Isaac had learned that the best way to handle liars was just not to give them the opportunity to lie. He would take a direct approach. "Darcy, we know you sent the blackmail letters," he told her.

She sat stock still. He could see the wheels turning in her head. How would she play this, he wondered.

"Your fingerprints are all over them," Isaac added.

She rolled her eyes. "Well of course they're all over the letters. I *gave* the letters to you. You *saw* me touching them. So what?"

"Darcy, your fingerprints are on the *undersides* of the letters," Isaac said, even though he hadn't had confirmation of that yet. "If you didn't create the letters, how did they get there?"

"I don't know," she said. "Maybe the blackmailer used clippings from magazines I had read. Yeah, they could have used magazines from the office." She glared at Isaac. "Have you talked with *everyone* in the office about this, or just me?"

"Darcy," Tom said. "We've talked with Gabe."

She stiffened. "Gabe? Gabe who?"

"Gabe Parrington," Tom said.

She bit her lip. She looked to the ceiling. She squeezed her hands tightly together in her lap. "Okay," she said more meekly. "But I was only trying to protect him."

"Protect him?"

"Yes. Meredith is a married woman! She was only playing with him. She needed to be stopped."

"So you were blackmailing her."

"Yes." She shifted in her seat. "She needed some incentive." And Darcy knew, deep down in her heart, that once Meredith was done with Gabe, he would come running back to her, and she could make it all better. If only… If only they hadn't had that unfortunate run in with her brothers at the restaurant that evening.

♦♦♦

It was only eight months ago when she and Gabe were out for dinner on their third date. She was already madly in love and was certain Gabe was the man for her. So certain, in fact, that she had chosen their wedding rings, tried on dozens of wedding dresses, and planned their entire wedding. She knew he was different from the others. They meant nothing. Gabe was all that mattered to her anymore. And she spent all her waking hours coming up with ways to make him love her. Make him want her. Make him stay.

But then those two miscreants snuck up to their table from behind her back. The taller one tapped Darcy on the shoulder. "Hey Sis," he said. "Long time no see."

Darcy turned, immediately rose to her feet, and started pushing them back and away while Gabe's mouth dropped open.

"What are you doing here?" she growled at them. "Get out of here."

"Hey, what gives?" the one with the beard exclaimed.

Darcy pointed toward the entry. "Get out of here and go back to the farm where you belong," she said.

The taller one frowned. "Really, Darcy?"

"Really," she snapped. "Get out of here. Now."

"Damn, Sis. That's cruel," the bearded man said.

The tall one looked over at his brother. "Comm'on bro," he said. Then he locked eyes with Gabe. "Watch out for her, man."

"Yeah," the bearded one agreed. He spun his finger around in a circle on the side of his head. "She's nuts."

Darcy slapped his hand down. "Out!" she commanded. She watched them leave, then retook her seat. "Don't mind them," she said with a wave of her hand. "Just two annoying pranksters I knew growing up. They always liked to give me trouble."

Gabe gave her a sideways look. "Pranksters? So, they're not your brothers?"

"No." Darcy smiled and reached across the table for Gabe. "Don't listen to them," she told him. "They're just idiots."

Gabe shook his head. "You know, Darcy, I can't believe a single word out of your mouth. First there was the pet collie you said you had, but don't; then the volunteer work you were supposed to be doing at the hospital, but no one there had ever heard of you; and now this? You told me you were an orphan." He folded his napkin and placed it on the table. "You know what? I just don't believe you. And I don't like the way you treated those men – whoever they were." He stood. "We're done," he said. And with that he left.

She tried to get in touch with him after that, but he ghosted her. She was sure that if he knew that the only reason she'd lied to him was because she loved him so much, he'd give her a second chance. That's why she followed him here to Minneapolis that day. That's why she followed Meredith to her home, and then to the gallery. That's why she got this job and started her blackmail plan.

◆◆◆

"So the blackmail was intended to give Ms. Stanton incentive to stop seeing Mr. Parrington?" Isaac asked.

"You can call her what she is, you know," Darcy barked. "She's *Mrs.* Stanton. A married woman! Back in the old days, she could have been stoned for what she was doing. She's the one who should be arrested."

"What have you done with the money?" Tom asked.

"The money?" Darcy almost started to laugh out loud at how easy it had been to take it. The first drop, when she was supposed to watch the drop-off site to see who picked it up, she just walked over and took it as soon as Meredith left, then sat in her car and read magazines until Meredith called. The second drop, she left the money in her car and pretended to deposit it in the trash can. That big raincoat made it as easy as pie. Meredith was so naïve. "I have the money," she said. "Has Meredith filed charges against me?" She smirked. "No, of course not. And she won't. She doesn't want her dearest love to find out she was having an affair." She used the air quotes around the words dearest love as she had become accustomed to doing. "She was the one being bad here. Not me."

It was a sentiment Isaac had heard far too often in his career. How one bad deed was not as bad as the other, thus making it somehow acceptable – even to the point of being righteous. "So, let's back up a bit. Just how did you end up being employed by Mrs. Stanton?" Isaac asked.

"I followed her to the gallery and noticed that there was a help wanted sign in the window, so I applied for the job."

"You followed her?" Tom asked.

"Of course. How else was I going to stop her?"

"Had you worked at other galleries before?" Isaac asked.

"No," she admitted. "But as long as I was willing to sign the waiver not to sue the gallery because of Artimus' obscene behavior, I was hired on the spot."

"I see," Isaac said. "Tell me about your relationship with Artimus."

"Just like everyone else, I tried to avoid him as best I could. But sometimes it took a slap or two."

Isaac raised his brows. "A slap or two?" he asked. Was that how he ended up in the pool, he wondered.

She crossed her arms over her chest. "Yes. That was encouraged at the gallery." She curled her lips up into a snarl. "He was such a letch."

Isaac sat back in his seat. If that was the way she felt about him, why would she visit his home, he wondered. Could Artimus have been in on the blackmailing as Meredith suggested or was it that Artimus found out about it and needed to be silenced. "Darcy, why were you at Artimus' home the evening he died?"

She blinked. "I wasn't." The heal of her foot began tapping the floor making her knee jump up and down. "Why would you even ask me that," she said. That wasn't the truth, but she wasn't going to confess to anything. She was certain she'd covered her tracks and there was no way they could ever find out she was there. Her eyes darted back and forth between Isaac and Tom. Or could they?

♦♦♦

That fateful night, the gallery had closed for the evening and Meredith had left in Darcy's car to meet up with Gabe, so Darcy pulled out the magazines and started finding and cutting out the words and letters she would need for the second blackmail letter. When she was just about finished, she was surprised to hear someone coming down the hall toward her office. Her heart started to race. Who could still be here? Did Meredith return for some reason? She stood to rush to the door to lock it, when Art leaned his bulky frame against the opening.

"What are you doing here so late, darlin'?" he asked. "Does that blonde have you working overtime?" He sauntered into her office, in that lumbering kind of way he had. "I'll have to have a word with her about that."

"Oh no," Darcy said as she nervously took her seat. "No need to do that." She started to push the scrap pieces from the magazine into the trash as discreetly as possible. "I'm just checking up on some things."

He grinned. "I'd like to check up on some things." he said as he leaned across to look down her shirt.

She put a hand to her chest and leaned back.

"Hey, what's all this?" he said, seeing the magazine clippings scattered on her desk. "Looks like some kind of ransom note." He laughed. "You plannin' on kidnapping somebody, sweetheart?" He held out his wrists to her. "'Cause you can take me for free."

Well, it was done, she thought to herself. There was no hiding it any longer. She rubbed her forehead. No hiding it from *Art*, anyway. She rubbed her chin. But just because Art knew, no one else needed to know, she reasoned. She looked up at him. It was in that moment of clarity she realized she would have to kill him.

She leaned back in her chair, placed her hands behind her head and stretched, the buttons on her blouse almost bursting at the strain. "It's a new art project I'm working on," she told him referring to the clippings on her desk. She released her arms and leaned forward. "I'd love to talk with you about it." She gently touched his arm. "If it's not too much to ask."

He grinned a lopsided grin. "Oh yeah, baby," he replied. "But it might cost you."

"Okay," she said. She smiled seductively. "Do you have time for a night cap?"

He licked his lips. "Yeah, I could fit that in. How about O'Connell's down the street?"

"Too noisy for me. Is there any place more private we can go?"

He winked at her. "Let's go to my place."

That's just what she wanted to hear. "Perfect. Give me fifteen minutes to finish up and I'll head over."

She completed the blackmail letter, cleaned up the scraps, and placed the letter in the mailbox. She arrived at Artimus' home a half hour later to find him well on his way to the bottom of his second scotch. Despite the heat, he led her to the pool patio.

"Feel free to jump in to cool off," he said.

"I might just have to do that," she responded, much to his delight. "But first let me fill that up for you and get one for myself."

He handed his glass over to her. "Please, help yourself," he said with a smile.

She grabbed a bowl and spoon from the kitchen cupboard and slipped into the bathroom. There she crushed ten Pronorfranil pills and slipped the dust into his drink. A few minutes later she was handing the doctored drink to him by the pool.

It didn't take long to take effect. She readied herself. All she needed to do now was strike him with a hard object. She panned the area and chose the chiseled rock statue of a naked woman that was sitting behind Art in the landscaping. She walked over to it, took off her blouse, and covered the statue with it. She leaned down and picked it up, finding it heavier than she expected. She carried it over and stood behind his chair. Just one whack on the head ought to do it, she thought to herself. She held it up and stood there for a moment, readying herself, but let the statue fall to her side. She just couldn't do it. She couldn't finish him off. She assured herself that he was so intoxicated he wouldn't remember all that had transpired, but she'd have to think of another way to explain away her "art project."

She put the statue back, cleaned up their glasses, wiped down everything she had touched and left as quickly as possible.

It seems the only thing she missed was the hand towel in the bathroom she used to wipe the Pronorfranil off the spoon she had crushed it with.

◆ ◆ ◆

"Darcy, we know you were there," Isaac said.

She breathed deeply like she had been taught to do when stress got the best of her, remembering how it had been welcome news hearing of Artimus' drowning, absolving her of the need to come up with excuses for what he saw. She looked down at the table so she wouldn't have to see their eyes. She had admitted to the blackmail, but not this. Never this. She put a hand on her knee to stop it from bouncing.

Isaac could practically feel a chill fill the air as she withdrew within herself.

"You're wrong," she said. "I wasn't there."

"A red corvette was seen leaving Art's home that evening."

"So?"

"So, we know you were driving Meredith's red corvette that night," Tom said.

"So?"

"So, why were you there?"

She crossed one leg over the other. "I wasn't," she said.

"Artimus ended up in the pool after an overdose of Pronorfranil," Isaac said.

Darcy leaned over and started drawing clockwise circles on the table with her finger. "So?"

"It was your Pronorfranil," Isaac said.

Her finger switched directions and went counterclockwise. "Not mine. I wasn't there."

"You didn't lose the pills down the gutter, did you?"

Her finger stopped momentarily. *How did he know that?* "I lost them down the gutter," she said, then moved her finger around clockwise again.

"Residue of it was found on the bathroom towel in Artimus' home," Tom told her. "How did it get there?"

"How would I know?" Her finger switched directions again. "I wasn't there."

Isaac and Tom continued with their questioning for another hour, while Darcy drew her circles. Try as they might, they were not able to get her to admit to being at Artimus' home that evening. She wouldn't budge.

It would take the forensics evidence to put her there.

CHAPTER 29

The autumn harvest moon sat on the horizon as Isaac pulled up next to the gallery. He parked in the very same spot he had parked in numerous times over the previous summer. 'Come as soon as you can,' Meredith's voice message began, then ended with the words, 'but no rush.' It was a rather cryptic invitation, but he had decided that the 'no rush' meant it could wait until the end of the workday.

He stepped out of the car and buttoned up his jacket to ward off the chill in the air. Things had certainly changed here over the last three months, he thought to himself. He stood for a moment, taking it all in. The once dark side of the building that had stored all of Artimus' paintings was now bright and open. A large ampersand had been added over the entrance door in the middle, and the word "Attitudes" had been added over the front window of the formerly dark side. *"Perceptions & Attitudes,"* he read aloud.

As he entered the building, the ringing of the bell over the door alerted Meredith that he had arrived.

She came toward him, arms wide open. "Detective. How good to see you," she said. "Thank you for coming!"

"You've really changed the space," he said as he shook her hand.

"Oh, yes! And I can't wait to show it to you." She clapped her hands together. "But first, can I get you a cappuccino? It's getting a little chilly these days," she added.

"That would be nice," Isaac said.

She spun on a heel and headed toward the café. Isaac followed. "Do you remember that we used to store Artimus' paintings over there?" she said and pointed to the right.

"I do," Isaac responded.

She moved around the counter and pulled out a couple of mugs. "Well, we revamped the basement level to keep the paintings in a new climate-controlled space there, so we could open up that side of the first floor." She placed one of the mugs under the Keurig machine. "Fiona,

Art's sister, is now using that space to create and sell her wearable art creations."

Isaac raised his brows. "Really?"

"Yes, and I'm wearing one of them." She did a little twirl causing the glitter to catch the light and sparkle.

Isaac had to smile at that, knowing that it was the very same glitter that ultimately convinced Darcy to plead to, and be convicted of, third degree murder. It was the same glitter the forensics team had determined was only available from a particular Italian company and was not widely used in the U.S; the same and only glitter that Fiona used for her clothing; and most importantly, it was the same glitter that was found all over Artimus' home.

Because even after Darcy had adamantly proclaimed that she had never, ever been to Artimus' house, that same glitter was found inside *her* home, and there was no way for her to explain that away. Simply put, every contact leaves a trace. It was the transference of the glitter that compelled Darcy to finally admit she had indeed been there. The actual charge brought against her was depraved-heart murder, a charge often used for drug-induced homicides. So, while there wasn't evidence to convict her of actually pushing Artimus into the pool, they had all they needed for this lessor charge. The motive had been to cover up the blackmail, and the Pronorfranil residue left on the guest bathroom towel and the red Corvette seen leaving the scene tied it all up in a bow. Cynthia was right that the key to solving the case was the antidepressant medicine, but the glitter was what locked it down.

"It's lovely," Isaac said somewhat surprised, remembering the slasher princess dress Fiona had been wearing when he first met her.

"Isn't it?" Meredith took the cup of steaming hot cappuccino and set it on the table for Isaac. "Here you go."

"Thank you," Isaac said.

"I think Fiona is really going to do well." The corners of her mouth turned up. "Now that she better understands her market, that is. You see, we had a long discussion about what her price point would need to be, and just who would be able and willing to pay it. Once she realized she should be marketing to a bit *older* age group, she made some…" Meredith paused looking for the right word. "Adjustments to her designs." She picked up her cup and beckoned with a wave of her hand. "Come on, let me show you the space."

Isaac followed. "It's so kind of you to take her under your wing," he said.

"Well, we figured it was only proper that Fiona inherit Artimus' contract for his percentage for the sale of his paintings, and she needed space for her wearable art endeavor, so things all sort of fell into place. Plus, I knew the first time I met her that she had a passion for her craft, and that I could help her succeed just as I did for Art." She put a hand to her heart. "Why, she's like a sister to me now."

Was that why she wanted him to come, he wondered. To see how things had worked out for the two of them? "I'm so happy things have worked out for the two of you," he said.

Meredith stopped in front of one of Artimus' paintings and gestured toward it. "Do you like it?" she asked.

This one was done in shades of blue. "Yes, I do," Isaac said. "I think it's one of the nicest I've seen."

"You know," she said, putting a hand on her hip. "I remember that you felt the color orange in the last painting you saw here evoked some kind of dichotomy." She looked over at him. "How would you describe this one?"

He took a moment to absorb it, trying to set aside the fact that it was just a painting of a floor tile. "Well, the color blue evokes feelings that are the opposite the color orange for me."

She nodded. "That's what I was hoping when I put it here."

"It's very peaceful," he continued.

"Good. Good," she said.

He cocked his head to the left. "This one conjures up memories of being a kid lying in the grass and looking up at a blue sky filled with wispy clouds."

"Oh yes, I see it!" she exclaimed. "That's just absolutely wonderful." She held out her hands and smiled at him. "It's yours."

"What?"

"It's yours," she repeated. "Take it. It's our way of thanking you for all you did for us."

A look of confusion appeared on his face. "But, oh my word, I was just doing my job. This is just so generous of you," he stammered, greatly overwhelmed by this act of kindness. "Thank you."

Fiona came up and stood by Meredith's side.

"Hey sis," Meredith said to her, and gave her a little squeeze.

Isaac noticed that not only had Fiona's dress designs matured, but her personal look had as well.

"Hey Detective," Fiona said. She pointed at the painting. "Like it?"

"It's amazing," he said.

"Meredith picked it out just for you," she told him.

"Oh my. That's so thoughtful. My wife will be ecstatic." He smiled wide and gestured toward Fiona's new space. "And it's great to hear how well all is going for you."

"Thanks," Fiona said. She looked up at her mentor's face. "Thanks to Meredith, my designs are really getting noticed."

"Awww, that's so sweet," Meredith blushed.

"I see the name of shop is *Attitudes*," Isaac said with eyebrows raised.

"Yeah, well, Meredith says I have a lot of it," Fiona said.

"And I *love* it," Meredith added.

Isaac laughed. "I guess it fits you, then."

"You should bring your wife in sometime," Fiona said. "I'll create something special for her – on the house."

"You see, Detective," Meredith said. "*Both* Fiona and I want to extend our gratitude." Her hands went to her heart. "I am especially grateful you were able to gather enough evidence so that the case avoided going to trial, thus keeping my personal business private."

"And I'm grateful that you found and convicted Art's murderer, so my reputation isn't in the gutter any more like it was after my interview with that witch, Mimi Winslow." Fiona put her hands on her hips. "I tell you, she'll <u>never</u> be wearing *my* designs – the big loser!" She drew out the word loser and held the shape of an "L" to her forehead. "And boy, will she be pissed about that." She slapped Isaac on the back. "Thanks, man," she said.

"That being said," Meredith continued. "We do hope that Darcy gets the help she needs."

"Yes, I do too," Isaac agreed. Darcy's mental health evaluation diagnosed her condition as a type of delusional disorder, and given this diagnosis, the court encouraged psychiatric treatment while Darcy served her sentence, but Isaac knew that individuals with mental illnesses were overrepresented in the prison population and that many prisons were just not equipped to provide the proper treatment.

"Yeah, she needs some serious help, that's for sure," Fiona said. She pointed to the back of the shop. "Good to see you, Detective, but I gotta go back and finish up my latest creation." A look of wonder came over her face. "It's for this crazy cool, old woman. Ha!" she laughed. "I mean she must be like a hundred or something."

Meredith pursed her lips. "More like in her seventies," she corrected.

"Well, whatever. The woman has style! A couple old ladies who saw my interview ordered dresses."

"Remember, Fiona," Meredith said to her. "They're not "old." They're "mature," "seasoned," or "venerable." *Never* describe them as "old.""

"Fine," Fiona acknowledged, petulantly. "Anyway, *however* you say it, pretty soon my designs will be all over town." Then she winked mischievously at Meredith. "But my next creation will be my very first *maternity* dress."

Meredith's grey eyes twinkled and she grinned wide.

Isaac turned toward Meredith. "May I ask?" He raised his brows. "Is this dress for you?"

She nodded.

"Well, congratulations," he said sincerely. "I'm so very happy for you."

"Thank you," she said. "And thank you again for keeping my confidential information, confidential."

Darcy had been right. Meredith did not file charges against her for the blackmail, and fortunately for the Stanton's, the judge agreed to seal the details of the blackmailing from the murder trial to protect the 'potential child.' "Your attorney made a good argument," Isaac said. He furrowed his brow. "How did Dirk take it?"

"Ah, well." She ran a hand through her hair. "He was understandably unhappy that I didn't tell him about my monthly meetings from the start, but he eventually also understood my reasons for being reticent to do so," she said. Her heart ached as she remembered getting home after the interrogation those three months ago.

◆ ◆ ◆

"Honey, can we talk?" Meredith had asked Dirk.

"Uh oh," he responded, because as all husbands know, the words "can we talk" usually means that bad news is on the way.

"No, no, it's good news," she told him, trying to put a positive spin on what was to come. "At least I hope you'll think so. Come. Let's sit down." She took a seat on the couch and patted the cushion next to her.

He joined her.

She folded her hands in her lap. "I have a confession to make," she began.

"That certainly doesn't sound like good news is forthcoming," he said.

She pulled the stray golden strands of hair back from her forehead. "Yes, well, just hear me out. It's a long story."

He sat back in his seat. "Of course."

She twisted the wedding ring on her finger. "Okay, well, several months ago when I was at the Mall of

America, I ran into a man who looked exactly like you." She tilted her head and smiled at him. "Well, not quite as handsome as you, but your doppelganger for sure."

"Oh?" he said, wondering where she was going with this.

"So, I showed him pictures of you, and he agreed; he looked just like you." She pulled her long ponytail to the front and wrapped a strand of hair around her finger. "Anyway, I couldn't help but think that his DNA would give us a child that looked like you – like it was ours." She stopped the twisting and looked at him with wary eyes. "So I asked him if he would be willing to donate his sperm to our cause."

Dirk's eyes opened wide. "Wow. That's a bold move."

She took his hands in hers. "Oh Dirk, I love you so much. I thought that running into him like that was a gift from Heaven. I wasn't going to just let him leave without at least asking."

"How did he take it?"

"He took some time to think it over and eventually agreed." She bit her lip. "So I had our attorney draw up an agreement.

He pulled away. "You talked to our attorney about this before you consulted me?"

She nodded sheepishly. "Yes, I'm so sorry. I wanted to see where this would go before consulting you. I know this is a difficult issue for you. So if it didn't work out, you wouldn't have to deal with it."

"You thought you were protecting me?" he squawked.

She cringed. "Yes." In the beginning, that was exactly what she had been doing. It had been heartbreaking for Dirk when they received the news that he would not be able to produce a family. He was in a funk for a very long time before Meredith convinced him that they could still have a family; that there were other ways. "I wanted to wait until the right time."

"The right time? *Right away* would have been the right time, Meredith."

She shifted in her seat. "You're right. I'm sorry."

"So he'll be giving his sperm to the Fertility Clinic?"

Meredith rubbed her temples. "Not exactly," she said. She took a deep breath, preparing herself for the hardest part. "Here's the catch. Our donor decided he would only agree to donate his sperm to us. Only us. No one else. He was uncomfortable leaving his sperm at the Fertility Clinic, out of his control. He felt that he could not be sure that, whether purposely or by accident, it could be given to someone else." This had been the biggest obstacle in their negotiations. This one condition almost derailed her dream. But she didn't let that happen.

"So it's over?"

"Well, no," she said. This was the moment she had been dreading. Because while she was certain running into Dirk's doppelganger was a gift from Heaven, she wasn't sure Dirk would share her feelings about what she was about to tell him. "You may or may not remember, but in our search for solutions as to how to become parents, I ran across a method for self-insemination."

"What?" he gasped. He stood and walked to the window.

She gulped. She needed to get through this. The whole story. She pushed her ponytail to her back. "So, I ordered the necessary equipment."

She could almost feel the heat start to emanate from his body.

He massaged the back of his neck. "I can't believe you haven't shared this with me."

"I'm so sorry," she whispered. The last thing she wanted to do was hurt him. He deserved to know, and she had been wrong to keep it from him.

He turned and glared at her. "And?"

"I scheduled an appointment with Mr. Parrington."

"Who?"

"Gabe Parrington. The doppelganger. The donor."

Dirk ran a hand over his head. "When is it?"

Her shoulders dropped. "The first appointment was in June."

"The *first* appointment?" He put his hands to his head as if it would explode if he didn't hold it together. "You mean you've already met with him? More than once?"

"Yes, since our agreement was signed, we've met twice now."

He crossed his arms over his chest. "I don't know what to say." He looked at the ceiling. "I'm just dumbfounded - and really, really hurt that you didn't share this with me."

Tears filled her eyes. "I know I was wrong. And Mr. Parrington was very clear that he would not participate without your approval."

"So you lied to him too? You lied to both of us?"

She let her head drop. "He never asked, and I never brought it up." In her own mind she envisioned it like creating a gift for Dirk. She focused on how happy they would be as a family. And what a miracle it would be to have a child that looked like it was his.

Dirk started to pace. "So how does this happen? Does he just hand over a vial or something?"

"Yes," she confirmed. "Then he leaves the room, and I insert it."

"He leaves the *room*?" he repeated with horror. "*Whose* room, Meredith?"

"His hotel room."

"His hotel room?!"

"Yes, but like I said, he just hands me the vial and leaves. Then I use his room while the process is taking place." She fidgeted with her bracelet. "It's best to lay prone after the injection, so I stay there for a few hours. Then I leave."

He blew out his cheeks. "Let me get this straight. You stay in his hotel room in his bed?!"

"It's not the bed he sleeps in; it's the other one."

His mouth dropped open. "Meredith, how do you know that?"

She sighed and held her palms to the sky. "I trust him."

Dirk rubbed his eyes, then the back of his neck. "I want to meet him."

"Yes," Meredith said. "That would be a good idea."

◆◆◆

"We had a wonderful heart to heart," she told Isaac. Wonderful may not have been the most accurate adjective for it, she thought to herself. Raw, authentic, and from the depths of their souls, would have described it better. It was certain that Dirk became more comfortable with the arrangement *after* meeting Gabe and being able to be a part of the process. But it was also certain that Meredith had made a dire mistake that would be difficult to undue. She had to come to grips with the fact that Dirk would no longer completely trust her, and that all the good intentions in the world could never replace honesty. In a voice full of lament but sprinkled with a tremendous amount of hope, she said. "I believe it will only serve to deepen our relationship."

They all stood there nodding for a moment, not knowing quite what to say.

Then Meredith smiled and placed a hand on her abdomen. "Of course, Dirk was very happy to hear this news."

"Ha!" Fiona chimed in. She gave Meredith a hug. "Not just happy, he was blissed out!

"That's great," Isaac said sincerely. "Blessings to you and your growing family."

"Thank you, Detective," Meredith said.

"Oh!" Fiona cried as a figure passed by the front window. "There she is!"

They all turned toward the door.

"Yoo-hoo!" she called out as she entered.

Isaac did a double take. "Edna?" he exclaimed.

ABOUT THE AUTHOR

Jennifer Anderson works in Minneapolis as a paralegal for a national law firm. She enjoys spending her free time with family and friends at their island cabin in northern Minnesota.

www.ingramcontent.com/pod-product-compliance
Lightning Source LLC
Chambersburg PA
CBHW071222210726
48293CB00002B/532